CHOSEN BY
ALPHA CLAIMED

NEW YORK TIMES and USA TODAY
BESTSELLING AUTHOR
MILLY TAIDEN

Piper Rain is a romance author that stopped believing in love. She's been unable to write about it since her divorce and having her heart broken. So she gets away and looks for inspiration out in the mountains. What she didn't expect to find was a sexy, romantic neighbor that would bring the spark of hope back into her heart.

Zain Lockwood is happy living out in the woods on his own. Though he is the alpha of a clan, he prefers solitude. Until a strong, beautiful but wounded female ends up as his neighbor. Suddenly, teaching her that love exists and that she is the perfect mate for him becomes his sole focus.

With problems with a neighboring Alpha and trying to find a way to romance Piper, Zain has his hands full. Piper's been emotionally hurt and she's not sure that she can love again. Even if it means letting go of the only man who's ever made her feel anything. But it all comes to a head when someone takes his mate. Zain will do anything to make sure Piper's safe, even if it means killing one of his own.

Published By
Latin Goddess Press
Winter Springs, FL 32708
http://millytaiden.com
Chosen by the Bear
Copyright © 2020 by Milly Taiden
Edited by: Tina Winograd
Cover: Jacqueline Sweet

❀ Created with Vellum

—*For those seeking a second chance at romance,*

Love will find you!

CHAPTER ONE

Piper Rain grumbled at the drops hitting her windshield nonstop. She should've waited until after the storm to go to the cabin, but she was tired of putting it off. Her mom had rented the place for a month for her. To help her be creative. Like that was going to happen.

Still, she didn't want to disappoint her mother, so she went. And now she was driving in the rain, or storm, at night, trying to find her way along the narrow mountain road. The GPS said she should be there soon—if it was even correct. The high hills in the area did a great job of blocking phone signals. Which was fine with her. She seldom used it.

It felt like she'd been driving from as high as

the clouds, down to as low as the bowels of hell, and back up in the middle of nowhere for hours already. Welcome to Ursuston, Blue Ridge Mountain Boonies, USA! But she didn't care. After all, what did she have to go back to? Nothing. She'd made sure to sign the divorce papers weeks ago. Long before she left on the trip.

The phone's ringing pulled her out of her pity party.

"Piper, darling," her mom's voice filled the inside of the Jeep. "Stop sulking."

She frowned and clenched her teeth. "I am not sulking, Mother."

"Of course, you are, dear. It's your nature. You hate losing and this marriage was a loss."

"Mom, this wasn't a game. This was my life. Ten years. Ten."

"I know, love, but you have to understand that Scott never saw you as anything more than a check."

"Gee, thanks." She sighed.

"Come on, love. You know I'm not trying to hurt your feelings. But when a man is only interested in you for money, then you know there's something wrong with the relationship."

"I know." And she did know. She knew damn

well what a worthless creep her ex-husband was. He'd created a business with her money and then hired someone to run it with him. Then he left her for that someone. One beautiful petite brunette with golden skin and a smile that Piper could never compete with.

She also couldn't compete with the bimbo's twenty-two years. Hell, Piper knew she wasn't ancient at thirty-five, but she was no perky college graduate with the body of a Barbie doll.

"Okay, then you also know this was not your fault. You do know that, right?" Her mother's voice was full of concern.

"I know that," she lied. She was still beating herself up over taking on so much work and forgetting to give Scott time. She'd all but shut him out in the last few years.

"Piper!" her mother snapped. "You and I know very well he's been cheating on you for years. This is just the point he decided he didn't need your money any longer."

Piper snorted. "Yeah. Apparently, his business is doing better than mine."

"That's only because you're burnt out, honey. And your creative side took a hit."

Yeah. More like exploded completely out of the

water. She didn't believe in love. Go figure. A romance author who couldn't write the necessary tropes for the genre. That was definitely going to create some problems for her stories.

If she could write. Which she couldn't because she was too busy being either angry or upset that her ex-husband had decided to use her for years for money but never bothered to give her the love and respect he'd agreed to at their wedding. But why was she mad at him? She was the one that allowed it to happen.

"Piper," her mother sighed. "you couldn't have known. Don't blame yourself. You were a wonderful wife to Scott. You encouraged him to do all the things he wanted. For half your marriage, he didn't do shit but laze around the house, and for the other half, he spent your money on himself, creating the business he wanted and never bothering to water the tree that gave him everything."

She sighed. She knew all that. All of it. But that didn't matter because all Piper wanted was to get away from everything. To forget Scott and his new fiancée. Yeah, he'd gotten engaged thirty minutes after he'd moved out and set a wedding date seconds after their divorce had gone through.

Her stomach rolled and anger threatened to boil over.

"Mom, I'm almost there. So I'll call you tomorrow. The weather is awful, and I want to stay focused on driving."

"All right, honey. Just be careful, please. And call me when you can."

"I will. Give me a few days, okay?" No sound came from the car speakers. "Mom?" Great. Signal gone again.

She hung up and gazed at the cabin in the woods that was supposed to be her sanctuary for the next thirty days. She sat in the car for a long time and gripped the steering wheel, staring at the lit cabin through her tears.

Why did she even care? It wasn't that she loved Scott. She'd stopped loving him a long time ago, but she'd made a commitment to be there for him. Which she'd done. But he'd never been there for her. Ever.

What hurt was that he never did any of the things with her that he was doing with his girlfriend. Oh, she'd heard from a mutual friend how he was taking her on dates and on his boat. They were doing so many outings and fun things together. But whenever Piper had asked him to spend any time with her, he'd been too busy. Or not in the mood.

She swallowed back at the knot in her throat and wiped away the tears. She wasn't going into that cabin with all that anger and bitterness in her heart. She'd never survive this and find her voice again if she did.

Scott did her a favor. It would've been worse if he strung her along another ten years before he did this. Though, she was mid-thirties, she could still enjoy her life, and hopefully, she could heal her heart enough that she could write again.

She opened the car door, grabbed her suitcase, and hurried through the rain to the front door. One suitcase. She'd packed only comfortable clothes to hang around in. Clothes to lounge and write in. And some to go into town to buy groceries if the need arose.

Surely there was a grocery store. On her way through the don't-blink-or-you-miss-it town, the place had one road: Main Street—and looked rundown. Almost ghost town-like with nobody outside due to the rain.

The security box attached to the log siding holding the key sat exactly where the written instructions said. It wouldn't have been the first time the information from the renter was wrong. Maybe this owner had some brains and cared for the place more than the dollars. She entered the passcode, pulled open the front plate, and took out the key. So far, so good.

Entrance open, she stood in the doorframe, suitcase dropping from her fingers. The inside of the massive cabin was surreal. Modern, yet, rustic. Rough-hewn beams crossed high overhead. From where she ogled the home, she could see all the way to the stainless-steel kitchen on the other side of the house.

Having the entire place to herself might be a bit intimidating. There could be another person in here the whole time, and she wouldn't even know.

Maybe in the guest room, a sexy man leaned against the bed's headboard, the sheet gathered in his lap. And under the sheet, a long hump that ran to the edge of the covers. His bare chest—

Piper shook her head to get rid of those thoughts. It was all fantasy, based on what she secretly desired from a guy. Her ex-husband never satisfied any of her fantasies, nor did he ever ask if she had any.

Another image popped into her head. One of the last scenes in Basic Instinct where Sharon

Stone was in bed with Michael Douglass, and she pulled a knife from the bedside. But instead of Stone, she lay there, and Douglass was her ex. Where the movie ended on a mysterious note, she wouldn't leave the reader in suspense.

Her ex would get a knife in his chest. Maybe two or ten times.

No, not really. She'd never stab him. All the blood would be a total mess. She'd just cut his brake lines like a character in one of her books.

She rolled her luggage through the living room to the stairs. The website said all the bedrooms were on the second floor with gorgeous views. Well, being that she could only see a few feet past the window, those sights would have to wait until tomorrow.

Choosing the first bedroom she came to, she laid her clothes on a chair and pulled jammies from her selection of outfits. Exploration of the house and surroundings would come in the morning.

CHAPTER TWO

Piper got up late the next morning after rolling around for the last couple hours. Too bad she was by herself. Usually, a man was connected to that bed—in her books, that was.

She glanced around the room and sighed. She'd barely slept. It was hard for her to relax in a strange bed and to feel comfortable in a new place. She was the type of person who disliked change. Lately though, it seemed that was all she was dealing with in her life. Nothing but change.

After showering and putting on leggings and a comfy sweater, she made coffee and climbed the stairs to the roof porch. The pictures on the website of this small wooden deck attached to the cabin's attic was one of the reasons she agreed to stay here.

And the views were worth the price. The rain had stopped, and as far as she could see, green coniferous trees filled the waving landscape. Though the river was down the hill, she had a clear view from where she stood. Last night, she heard the rushing water as the rainfall swelled the riverbed. She wondered where the waterfall mentioned in the rental add was.

Taking a deep breath, she noticed the air smelled different than in New York. Could that be clean, fresh air she scented? How novel was that?

She remembered the news reports a couple years back about the forest fires in the Blue Ridge Mountains. The blazes here weren't nearly as bad as those in California. The television clips from here showed the higher ridges burning, most fires started by lightning.

Thank god she didn't have to worry about infernos on the mountain. On the contrary, the Weather Channel predicted rain for several days. Not that she'd let that ruin her time off.

She hadn't had a vacation in a long time. Too long. Scott hadn't been into going anywhere with her. He'd always used the excuse that he hated getting on planes to not do things with her. She drank her coffee and sighed.

Her heart was still raw from the rejection. And, dammit, she wasn't even that heartbroken. When she married Scott, she'd felt he was a nice guy and decided marrying him had to be a good step for her.

He claimed that he loved her. How lucky could she be finding someone who cared for her. Some people never found love. Even if she didn't love him at the time of the wedding, she figured after some time, she would come to love him.

That would be a big nope. She'd settled for what she thought was the right choice and instead ended up feeling half empty most of her marriage. So when he told her he wanted a divorce because he fell in love, she felt as if he'd slapped her in the face.

How many times had she asked herself what was wrong with her marriage? With her relation-ship? Too many. But then she'd tell herself nobody led a perfect life and that Scott was a good man. She snorted. Right. A good man, her ass.

She drained the rest of her coffee and decided to go for a walk. It was a beautiful day, and though chilly, the sun was out, and she really needed to get some air. She'd been locked away in a city apartment, hiding from the world for too long.

Once she had her hiking boots on, she slipped on a jacket and put her phone, a water bottle, and handful of ribbon strips in her pocket. She wanted to look for the waterfall. The sound of the running river soothed her. She'd seen a trail that led from the back of the cabin down to the river. She followed it, glancing around and loving the views.

The outdoors had never really been her thing. She was more of a nice hotel type of person, but only when she did the paying, which was always. She'd rather spend money at a spa or hotel with great room service rather than exploring. But at that moment, walking through the woods felt perfect.

Never in her life had she expected anyone to give her expensive gifts or treat her to outrageous vacations. She worked hard so she could give herself those things. Besides, when it came to others, she truly believed the thought was what counted.

Scott had never really given her gifts. He'd handed her money to buy herself flowers and whatever she wanted for holidays. It made her angry just thinking about it. His excuse was always he didn't know what she might like or want. But really, she believed he just didn't even want to try.

Staying on the bank and tying a ribbon on the tree next to the trail that led back to her cabin, she continued to walk down the hill, marking her way as she went. Small critters dashed here and there, scurrying to find food for the winter quickly approaching.

She felt a little like that. She knew what she had to do for her future, but the damn writer's block was the size of an iceberg. For the first time in her professional career, she didn't feel like writing. No number of words on the page or images in her head brought inspiration. Her muse had been beaten up, kidnapped, tortured, and killed. Geesh, overdramatic much?

By the lack of breath in her chest, she was severely out of shape if walking downhill made her feel like she was dying. She frowned, stopped by a tree stump and sat to catch her breath. Pulling the water bottle out, she took several long gulps and glanced around. The area was quiet and peaceful. The rushing water was all the noise she heard.

About to turn around and head back, the sound of crying called her attention. She frowned. Crying? Listening intently, she realized she'd been holding her breath waiting for the noise. Then she heard it again. It was crying. It sounded like a child. She did a full circle, looking for who made the noise, but didn't see anyone.

Instinct told her to find the child. She couldn't live with herself if a little kid was lost in the woods and she left him or her out there. Rushing farther down the hill, she listened until the crying drew closer. Then she stepped off the path into the trees and saw her. The little girl couldn't be more than four or five years old.

"Hello?"

The little girl wore a yellow raincoat covered in bright red lady bugs and holes large enough to render the covering useless. Her wet pigtails were sagging off her head and her face was covered in tear streaks cutting through dirt. She stared wide eyed at Piper.

"Hi," Piper said softly. "Is that you crying?"

The little girl nodded and then hiccupped.

"Why?" She stepped closer to the little girl. When the child took a step back, she said, "Don't be scared. My name is Piper. Maybe I can help you. Are you lost?"

The little girl's lip trembled, and her eyes filled with tears.

"Oh, honey, don't cry. It will be okay." From the inside coat pocket, she pulled a half-eaten protein bar. "Are you hun—" The child tore the food from Piper's hand and shoved it into her mouth. If Piper hadn't taken the wrapper off, the girl might have eaten that too. How long had she been out here? "What's your name?"

"E-Emma."

Piper squatted in front of Emma, something her thighs would regret later, but she didn't want to scare the little girl. "Where did you come from?"

Emma glanced around and then sniffed. She pointed behind her, farther down the hill.

Piper groaned as she stood and offered Emma her hand. "Come on, I'll help you find your parents."

Emma stared at the offered hand for a moment before sniffing again. She blinked at Piper, her gaze full of concern, but then took her hand with her much smaller one.

They started down the hill, looking around for other people.

After several minutes of seeing no one, Piper asked, "Are you sure we're going the right way?" She wondered if the child really knew the direction to where her mom and dad were.

"Yes."

"You don't talk much for a little kid. How old are you, Emma?"

Emma glanced up at her with her big honey brown eyes. "Almost five, but I can't have a party."

Piper grinned. "Why not?"

Emma nodded. "Momma said it wouldn't be a propate."

"Not appropriate, huh? Well, we are going to make sure that you get to your momma and your daddy very soon."

"Do you like dolls?" the high-pitched voice said.

Piper laughed at the question. "I do. When I was little like you, I had this cool doll that you could put make up on and take it off with a little wet cloth."

Emma's brows lifted and her eyes filled with surprise. "Makeup?" She glanced down at her little red tipped fingernails and then back at Piper. "I like makeup but don't have any since we moved."

"I bet you do, sweetie," Piper replied, only half listening. A loud sound came from within the trees, but she didn't see animal or human. It was a big roar. The hairs on her arms stood on end and fear clutched at her heart.

The ground vibrated like a bass drum played in

a parade. She pushed Emma behind her when she saw a massive bear coming out of the woods, its eyes on her. She continued pushing Emma back up, the at the same time trying to keep her behind her.

"Uh-oh. He's angry," Emma said.

Angry? That beast looked ready to kill. Fear clutched a fist around Piper's heart. The bear lifted onto two legs and roared again. The bottom of her stomach dropped. She shoved Emma back. "We need to go, honey. I won't let him hurt you."

The bear dropped onto all fours and she took her chance, picked up Emma and started running upriver. The bear huffed and chased them. She glanced over her shoulder and saw it gaining on them. She stopped and shoved Emma forward. "Keep going, Emma. I'll stop it."

Had those words really come out of her mouth. How the hell was she going to stop a charging bear without looking like lunch for the creature? Of all her stories, never had one of the characters faced a bear. She knew what to do in case of dog attack, elephant charge, and being bitten by a poison snake. All she could do was stand there to give Emma time to get away.

Less than a yard in front of her, a second,

bigger brown bear slammed into the first one, sending it to the edge of the river. She slapped a hand on her chest and struggled to catch her breath while watching the two bears fight. The bigger one shoved the smaller bear and tossed him against a tree. They roared back and forth, slapping and punching each other.

Piper watched, horrified, as the two bears clawed at each other's muzzles and bit each other's faces. The roaring sounds tripped her heartbeat and the slams against the trees shook the ground.

The big bear shoved the smaller one onto his back, smacking the other's attempts at biting him. They moved so fast, it was hard to keep up with. They were all over the place, clawing at each other. The bigger bear tossed the other at another tree. He slammed it hard, making a loud cracking noise.

Then the big bear smashed the little one on his back again, but the smaller animal wasn't having it. He kicked the other bear back and tried to claw at his face and bite him. Though the bigger one had the upper hand with size and speed, the smaller guy seemed determined to get him.

"Stop!" Emma screamed. "Stop! Stop! Stop!"

Piper's eyes popped wide as she looked over her shoulder to see the girl not far away. Why hadn't she run? The two bears separated and moved away from each other. She glanced at Emma's pale face and teary eyes. "How did you—"

"Daddy!" Emma called out with a soft cry. "Daddy, don't fight!"

To Piper's amazement, the smaller bear shifted into a human man. A naked, very angry-looking, human man. She slapped a hand over her mouth and gasped. Holy fuck! What the hell was going on?

Then, the bigger bear shifted into a tall, buff man straight out of her dirtiest dreams. With wild hair and a sexy beard, he had the look of what she expected a mountain man out of a porn movie might look like.

Oh, and he was naked. So fucking naked. His body was all golden-brown muscle with strong legs and...whoa. She didn't just stare at his dick. She tried to glance away but couldn't. Yeah, she'd stared. Fuck. She was still staring. She couldn't look away. He was massive. Who was this guy?

"Daddy!" Emma whimpered.

Piper glanced at the two heaving males, unsure what to do. Piper's vocal cords had stopped working. She'd never met a shifter, much less seen a fight between two.

The smaller man gave her the evil eye and then turned to the bigger guy. "Stay away from my property, Zain." He glared at Piper. "And your guests too, or the next time I see someone taking off with my daughter, I won't stop until they're dead."

Piper gasped and slapped her hands on her hips, ready to argue with the man, but stopped when she saw Emma watching her. She didn't want the little girl scared any more than she already was.

"Take your daughter home, Ali. I'm pretty sure nobody was trying to steal your child."

Ali growled. His eyes flashed a bright gold and then he marched away with Emma in his arms. The man walked away naked like it was no big deal.

"Are you okay?" Hunk of muscles asked.

"I-Yes. I think so." She frowned. "I'm sorry, did I just see you both go from bear to human or do I need to call my doctor and tell him I'm seeing things?"

A grin spread over his lips and he chuckled. "No need to ask if you've lost your mind. We're shifters. Ali belongs to the South River Clan and I am alpha of the Black Peak Clan." He offered her his hand. "Zain Lockwood."

"Uh," she gulped, unsure if she should take his hand, but did anyway. You know, all that disease and shit floating around. She could barely think straight now that he'd come so close. He was talking to her as if it wasn't a big deal to walk around with his junk hanging out the trunk. "I'm, uh, Piper. Piper Rain."

"Piper. I like that."

"Thank you. Where is his land that he said he didn't want anyone trespassing on? I didn't see any no trespassing signs."

He pointed down river. "About two hundred yards. There aren't any signs."

Around the spot she'd found Emma crying. "You know, I didn't trespass to steal his kid. I heard Emma crying and was going to help her find her parents."

He shrugged. "Ali and his clan are very argumentative. They like to start trouble, so they assume someone is always looking to fight."

She frowned and cleared her throat. "I, uh, guess I should be going back."

"You're up at the top river cabin, right?" he asked, his gaze roaming her face.

She nodded and forced herself to look at his face and not venture south. No matter how much her brain kept telling her to. He really had a great face with a strong jaw, long dark lashes curled around chocolate brown eyes, and a beard that made her girl parts wake from hibernation. His eyes twinkled with humor.

"I should go," she said. "Thanks for coming to the rescue. Seriously."

"No problem. I'm the caretake of that cabin. I'm sure my name and number are on your contact information."

She gasped. "That's right! I did see a Zain name on my contact email."

He nodded. "If you have any other issues, feel free to come by. I'm close to you, just follow the path from the backyard that goes into the woods instead of coming down by the river. It goes straight to my place."

Piper nodded and turned to go. Her face was hot enough to boil water. She couldn't stand there and talk to the cute *naked* man like it was natural. It wasn't. Nothing about this meeting was normal.

CHAPTER THREE

When Piper got back up to her cabin from her action-packed walk in the woods, she glanced at her laptop and sat to make notes. But when it came time to do some of a story, her fingers froze on the keys. *It's okay. It's normal. Don't push it and don't rush it.*

Fucking hell! She needed to write again. Not only because it was her job and she did that for a living. She had deadlines to meet. But more importantly, writing was her escape. Throughout her failed marriage, it was what kept her going on a daily basis.

When sexual frustration or frustration from life in general became too much, she jumped into another world where the men were perfect, and the women kicked their asses for the shit they tried to get away with. The desires and temptations expressed on the page poured out of her soul. She wouldn't tell anybody this, but she lived vicariously through her characters.

Without her imagination, her life would've been hell. And she would've needed way more meds. She was on anti-depressants as it was. No pill gave her the same thrill as living through the fictional lives she put through shit to get their happy ending.

Was that the fate of her own life? To go through shit to achieve her happily ever after. In her case, she doubted her story would end like those she wrote. A girl could hope, right?

Exasperated, she schlepped to the kitchen and made herself a sandwich for lunch and then picked up a paperback. Horror was one of her favorite things to read. It always seemed to help her find her muse, and she truly liked reading creepy shit. It felt cathartic, in a way. Get the shit scared out of you, and you forget about your problems while you're peeking around the door to make sure a killer isn't behind it waiting for you.

The rain had started again. The wind howled and rain pelted the roof. She didn't mind the drops. A thunderstorm was one of the few noises she could put up with when she wrote. The sound was soothing and made her sleepy.

Then suddenly, she was in the dark. Great. Power outage.

She picked up her phone and hit the flashlight button. Panic rose inside her. The cabin was huge, and her little light didn't uncover enough of that dark space. She sat quietly, waiting for the lights to come back on.

She heard a creak overhead. Her heart flipped. Was that caused by the footstep of a crazed murderer who'd escaped prison and been on the run for weeks? Maybe it was a bear shifter with a rather large human package that she'd like to get her hands, and mouth, on.

She imagined herself climbing the stairs to the bedrooms as silently as she could. Another footfall would freeze her on the spot. The smell of the woods after a rain filled her nose. Despite the reader yelling for her not to go up there, she continued. She had to know who or what was in the cabin with her.

As she reached the top, one of the doors clicked open. He was there. Dammit, she should've gotten a knife before going up. Didn't matter. This was her story and she could simply kick his ass and throw him out the window if she wanted.

Slowly, she pushed the door open and stepped inside. The room was dark except for a candle sitting in the middle of a dresser. Music with a soul beating tempo floated on the air. Where did that come from? No, cut that—too cliché. Her editor would chew her another butthole for using something so blasé.

The small flickering flame called to her. Almost in a daze, she glided to the candle. In the mirror on the dresser, she saw him. Muscles defined down his shoulders and arms. His slick chest was broad above a perfect eight pack. Six was too common. Eight would be the right amount for her hero. Maybe she'd do some research to make sure. Her readers were smart and would call her out if she got it wrong.

His perfectly sculpted arm wrapped around her waist, pulling her against him. Oh god, he was hard as steel on her back side. She couldn't breathe, hadn't breathed since she'd walked into the room. He'd murmur something dirty sending fire straight to her lower stomach. Oh yeah, this was going to get hot. If she could only put this on paper.

His hand slid under shirt, cupping her bare breast, tweaking the—

A solid *thunk* came from the kitchen porch area.

"Oh, fuck," she said, snapping out of her mind. Her heart really was pounding. Another noise—like a deck chair being scooted across the wood deck—got her to her feet. That was too deliberate to have been the wind. The chair would've blown over, not be dragged away. Someone was seriously out there.

What if that Ali guy came back to kill her for taking off with his daughter? He was as pissed as a wet chicken—cliché again. *Get a fucking grip, Piper!* This wasn't a thriller plot line.

Maybe not, but she rushed to the kitchen and pulled out a butcher knife from the block. Why always a butcher knife? Why not a mixing spoon or potato peeler. Yeah, okay, a butcher knife it was.

Her heartbeats tripped over each other as she held her breath. She listened intently but only the storm raged outside.

Creaking sounded from above. Fuck, were there two of them? Her heart was ready to pop out of her chest. Why the fuck did she choose to read horror while alone in a cabin, in woods, in the middle of nowhere? Wasn't that always where the murders happened? Jesus, she was being dumb and deserved to get murdered.

She hugged the wall, sliding to the door leading out back. Another creak right in front of the entrance. Was the door locked? Of course not. What kind of idiot stayed alone in a cabin, in the woods, in the middle of nowhere and left the freaking door unlocked? Well, hell. That'd be her.

Piper gripped the knife harder. She had two choices. One—she confronted the killer head on. Show him she wasn't scared shitless alone in a cabin, in the woods, in the middle of nowhere with the freaking door unlocked. Her editor would cut that too. Repeated verbiage.

Two—she could run to the other side of the house, throw open the door to see lightning split the tree a few yards from the cabin. Half of the trunk would explode from the tree, sending it straight for her. She'd be too frightened to move and the branches would pierce her body, killing her instantly.

Well, choice one sounded like the better of the two.

Using the element of surprise, she yanked the door open and screamed at the sight of a dark figure standing there. Christ on a pogo stick, there was someone trying to get in. She had to kill or be killed. Her arm thrust forward.

"It's me!" the person yelled over her screaming and grabbed her swinging hand, stopping her from stabbing him. "Me, Zain. I came to help get the generator running."

"What?" She swallowed big gulps of air and tried to stop the dizzying sensation in her head. The fear and adrenaline in her blood had her ready to jump out of her skin. "Zain. Fuck, dude. Don't you know how to knock?"

He chuckled. "I was about to when you opened the door. I thought you saw me."

"How the hell could I see you? I mean, there are windows everywhere, except right here by the door where I can't see you!" she gasped. "Plus, I wouldn't recognize you in clothes."

He threw his head back and laughed. Yup, she'd know who he was if his junk was hanging out, but all bundled up, she wouldn't have known.

Oh god. She hadn't meant it like that, but that was basically the truth. She couldn't forget what sights her eyes had seen.

She shook her head. "Never mind. The electricity is off. So don't hurt yourself."

He stepped inside and stood on the door mat, dripping wet. Oh fucking donuts, he looked good. Henley-style shirt clinging to every muscle. His arm lifted, flexing his bicep and chest, to run his big, strong hand through his wet hair, pulling it back from a face with dark eyes and lips that she could kiss forever.

"Uhh," he said, standing there. "Let me go downstairs and get the electricity back on for you."

She nodded and held on to the countertop for dear life—from fear or lust, she wasn't sure. One thing was for certain, she'd aged twenty years in the span of hours. First the bear chasing her and now the crazy owner trying to pull a Norman Bates on her. But she was the one holding the knife.

She'd just gotten her heartbeats and breathing under control when the electricity came back on. She sat at the dining table and shook her head. How was she supposed to relax like this?

"Are you okay?" he asked, coming up from the basement. His top outlined his upper torso, but somehow, she found herself staring at his crotch as if willing his pants to disappear.

Her head and eyes snapped up. "I'm good. Just reading too much horror."

He grinned again. That smile was dazzling, lighting up his face, putting a slight squint to his lids. "You sure you should be reading that while you're alone in a cabin in the woods—"

"In the middle of nowhere with the freaking door unlocked," she finished, then grinned at herself and shook her head.

He stared quietly at her for a moment, not moving one of those hunky muscles. "Uh, right. The worst of the storm has passed," he said. "I guess I'll leave you to it."

"Wait!" She should let him go, but she didn't want to. So what if she was afraid of her own shadow right now. She didn't want to be alone after the noises she'd heard upstairs. "Would you mind checking the cabin with me? I'll repay with a cup of coffee."

His eyes flashed gold. "I'll stay if you want me to."

What else would he do if she asked really nicely? Horny much?

"Please. I haven't really checked all the rooms to make sure there's no other person staying here at the same time."

He chuckled and shook his head. "You're here alone. I checked the cabin before you arrived."

She raised her brows. "Really? You just didn't leave it the way the previous person left it? Trashed out and stuff?" The place was immaculate so why she said that was beyond her.

"Of course," he answered, wrinkling the area between his eyes. "This is my mother's cabin. She rents it out when she travels. Right now, she and my aunts are on a cruise around the world."

"Oh. Wow. This is a big cabin for just your mom."

"She really hasn't lived here in over a year. When my father died, she had a hard time coming back here. So she started traveling and has been gone ever since. It sat empty until someone suggested I rent it out."

She winced. "I'm so sorry about your dad." She bit her lip and wrung her hands together. Should she ask him to stay again? No, he was a stranger. Yes, he was hot as hell in a matchbox. No, he. . . "What about some coffee?"

"I'd love some."

Thank god. "Sit. I'll make it. I also saw a cake in the fridge when I made a sandwich earlier."

"Yeah. It's there. Chocolate."

She laughed and glanced at him from the fridge. "You want a piece?"

"I definitely want a piece." A sneaky grin spread on his face.

She met his gaze and gulped. Cake. He wanted cake. Right?

CHAPTER FOUR

Zain Lockwood watched his mate, Piper Rain, cut him a piece of cake and set it on a plate. She was beautiful, but he saw pain in her features. There was so much sadness in her eyes and her glances were guarded.

Damn, he couldn't believe she just suddenly walked into his life. And a human. His mother would be having kittens if she were here. She'd always told him to not have serious relationships because when he found his true mate, he'd leave the other heartbroken. And being the next alpha, he didn't want anyone mad at him.

He really didn't need or want a mate right now. Not long ago, he found a way to connect with the younger generations and that was his focus. Not to mention the ongoing repairs and maintenance of the decrepit town. But there she was. His mate.

Piper placed a pot of coffee, cream and sugar bowls on the table and handed him a cup.

"Thanks," he said.

She nodded and rushed back to get the cake, spoons, and forks. "So do you get lonely up here?" she asked.

He took the cake plate from her hand, noticing the tremble of her fingers as he grazed hers with his. Their gazes met. She licked her lips, quickly looked down at the table and sat.

"I like solitude. I have a sleuth down the mountain, in the heart of Ursuston. Black Peak is our home."

"Sleuth, that the same as a clan?" He nodded as she added sugar and cream to her coffee. "I hadn't heard of that term before. And, yeah, I drove through your cozy little home on my way up here."

"It must've looked deserted when you passed through. Everyone was home by then."

"Yeah. It was kind of creepy. Reminded me of that movie *Wrong Turn*."

He laughed even though he could tell she was serious. But it was hard not to find her amusing with her continued references to horror movies and being scared. "I think you should start watching and reading something other than horror."

She grinned and took a bite of cake. Then she closed her eyes and moaned. "Mmm."

"It's good cake."

Her eyes popped open. "Good? Are you crazy? That cake is amazing. Who made it? I'll have to bribe her for a recipe."

He spooned sugar into his coffee. "I made it."

She stopped the fork midway to her mouth. "Yeah, right." She laughed and ate her cake. "It's so good. Really, though. Who's the baker?"

"I am. Really." He chuckled at her shock. "My aunt owns the bakery in town. It's called Clarice's Cakes. I used to spend a lot of time with her when my parents were downtown at meetings and I wasn't allowed to be there as a kid. So I learned to bake a few things. This one is her world famous chocolate cake. One day, she said she was going to teach me," he laughed.

He watched her eat another piece of cake and she did a little groan that made him want to see her in the throes of pleasure. "So she taught me, and I make it whenever I want cake."

"I would've never guessed."

"Don't get too excited, "he told her. "I only know how to make three things. My big thing is the grill."

She blinked. "You mean you cook too?"

"Come on, it's grilling. All men know how to grill. Slap it on, turn it over, set it on fire, then it's done."

"Not where I'm from. Then again, I don't really know many men. The ones I do know don't cook or bake."

He heard the bitterness and edge in her words. "You seem a little angry about that. Want to talk about it?"

She frowned, sighed, and shook her head. "Sorry. I'm still a little upset about my divorce, I guess."

His heart clutched. Knowing she was his mate was one thing, but pursuing a woman who was in love with someone else was not really his thing. "I'm sorry."

She waved her hand in dismissal. "It's all good. He was an asshole who's getting married to a perky college grad as we speak." She met his gaze. "I'm not even in love with him. I haven't really loved him in years. I was loyal and faithful and caring even when I felt empty inside." Her shoulders dropped. "It doesn't matter. We've been divorced for three months and this anger resurfaces when I least expect it."

He nodded. "That's still rough. You dedicated your time to someone, and it didn't work out. It's understandable to be going through a range of emotions."

Her brow furrowed. "Really? Is it? My mom and my family and friends are making me feel like I'm supposed to forget it all and move on yesterday." She rubbed her temple. "Don't get me wrong, I am looking forward to moving on and having a hopefully more fulfilling life now, but they act like I'm not supposed to feel anything after ten years of marriage has gone down the drain."

Fuck. Ten years. He saw the strain in her face and the haunted look in her eyes. "Nobody can tell you how to feel, Piper."

Her features smoothed out and a smile tipped her lips up. "Thank you. That's really understanding of you. I wish more people got that."

There was a moment of silence and he watched her stare at his mouth. The sweet scent of her desire filled his chest. Fuck. She might be upset over her divorce, but he at least had a chance with her. It might take time to get her to let go.

"Do you want me to turn the fire on for you?"

She blinked and nodded, her pupils dilated, and her lips slightly parted with a small grin. "Yes, please. Light my fire."

Fuuuck. He didn't expect that type of invitation.

CHAPTER FIVE

Zain was busy thinking of all the ways he could get his mate to relax while he turned on the logs in the living room.

"I love this sofa," Piper said behind him.

He glanced over his shoulder and saw her lounging on one of his mother's favorite pieces. The massive sofa had many parts, that when placed in different ways, could make a bed or a big closed-in sectional to be shared among a lot of people. Currently, the sofa was set up in a large C with ottomans that extended the front to give the whole thing a big bed feel.

"Yeah, I love that sofa too." He finished with the fire and sat next to her. She had the remote in her hand and flipped through movies on demand.

"Is there anything you want to watch?" she asked.

Was he really hearing this? Maybe it was his too hopeful imagination. "You want me to stay?"

She blinked at him and nodded slowly. "I mean, unless you're busy? I didn't realize how lonely it could get up here by myself. Normally, when I'm writing, I can be in total quiet all day, but with my creative side broken, I'm not feeling all this being alone stuff."

He stretched his feet out on the big sofa. "What do you write?"

A deep blush took over her pale features. "Romance."

"Nice."

She glanced away from the TV and looked at him. "That's it? You're not going to make some dirty joke about mommy porn in books and all that?"

"No. Why would I? My mom loves reading romance. Reading got her through some of the hardest moments after my father died. Whether it's romance, horror, action or thrillers, a book is a book. And the same effort goes into any type of book." He frowned. "Except maybe history. Those people need to be pretty accurate with their details, so I'll say they might give some extra effort."

She laughed and nodded. "You're right. I couldn't write a historical for the life of me, but, boy, do I love to read them. Well, used to." She sighed. "I haven't read anything romantic in a long time. I've been struggling writing this past year, but I am ahead with my work, so I didn't worry too much that books were taking longer. Then epic writer's block. I couldn't write anything."

He raised his brows. "Anything?"

"Nothing. I'd sit there and stare at the computer. It's been horrible. Going through the divorce and all that. It has really killed my romantic side." She shrugged. "I stopped believing in love. How can I write about something I don't think exists?"

He turned to her on the sofa and grabbed her hand. "I understand you're dealing with something difficult, but you can't let it stop you from believing in love."

She glanced down at their hands and then at his eyes. "I'm here to find my voice again. To figure out who I am as an author and maybe even to figure out who I am as a woman. But with everything I've lived through in my marriage, I really have a hard time believing in love and romance, and sometimes even in myself."

"Well, we'll just have to figure out a way to help you believe again," he told her, his voice firm.

She smiled again. He loved seeing her smile. Her eyes lit up and her face seemed to glow. "You're funny, but unrealistic."

"Are you challenging me?"

She laughed this time. "It's not a challenge, Zain. I've been kicked in the face too many times by the very thing I write about. Love. My heart is bruised, and I don't know if I want to believe in it anyway. Safer without it."

"Why is it so hard to think that love can happen again for you."

She let out a loud exhale. "I don't know. Maybe because I realized I was never in love with Scott. So that means that this whole time what I thought was love wasn't. Then I must not know what it is." She curled her feet under a cushion. "Look, all I've seen of romance is men spending money left and right buying women stuff. Stuff that they don't even need or want. How is that romance?"

He nodded. "You're right. That's not romance."

"Exactly. And my own ex used money to show me love. How is a new purse or a new bracelet going to show me love?" She bit her lip. "I don't know what I'm supposed to see in all this, but I don't think any of what I've experienced in my life is real love. My father passed away when I was too young to remember, but my mother often talks of how much they loved each other and how great a husband he was."

She squeezed his hand. "But my parents come from wealthy families. Showing love with material objects is normal for them. And even then, my mom says stuff took a back seat to doing things together."

"Stop thinking so hard, Piper," he said and captured her chin in his hand. He watched her eyes widen as he leaned forward. "Give your brain and heart a break. Just let them heal."

He wanted to kiss her more than anything, but he sensed she wasn't ready for it. Fuck, it was tearing him up inside. His bear wanted a taste of his mate, but he wanted her to see he wouldn't push her. They could go at her pace. He'd let her lead the way. Even if it killed him.

CHAPTER SIX

Piper chose a random horror movie she'd seen several times and clicked it to play. He slipped off his boots and leaned back, getting comfortable. She shouldn't be suckering Zain into staying with her, but she really liked his company. He was nice and understanding. The fact that he was hot as balls and made her stomach flip wasn't even part of the equation. Not much, anyway.

"So what do you do?" she asked him, wanting to know more about the tall, sexy mountain man.

"I build furniture," he said. "My father created a company with my grandfather a long time ago where they built custom furniture and in the era of the internet, they had a massive boom once their pieces made it online. I was his apprentice as a kid, but now I make the pieces for the company."

"Really?" she asked with interest. "What's the company name?"

"Lockwood and Son."

"Seriously?" She gasped. "I know nothing about furniture, but I know your store. All my mother's friends rave about your custom pieces. They said they're on a waiting list to get something made by you."

He grinned. "I don't take on too many projects at a time. I like to give my attention to whatever I'm working on."

"Wow. That's...that's freaking amazing."

"You're the bestselling romance author and you're making it sound like it's the other way around."

She blinked. "You have no idea how the world of socialites in New York is. The fact that all those women know your work is definitely a big deal. I bet your mom is super proud of you."

"Yeah. She is. We don't discuss it much. She's still healing from losing my dad."

"I'm sorry, Zain. I bet you miss both of them. I mean, he's gone, and she's decided being here is too much. So it's like you lost them both."

He nodded. "Feels like that a lot of the time."

They watched the movie in silence after that. She felt guilty for bringing up his parents and then anger that his mother had abandoned him. Sure, she needed to grieve, but to forget her son and just take off like that? Who did that?.

She woke to the sound of rain and howling wind again. She didn't realize she'd dozed off and ended up cuddled up into Zain's side. Taking a moment to glance at him, she realized she felt more comfortable with this man than she ever had with Scott. Zain's arm held her protectively to him and his breathing was deep and steady.

Raising a hand from his chest, she lightly touched his beard and drew her finger slowly over his lips. His eyes popped open and he grabbed her hand before she could take it back.

"Hi," she whispered.

"Hi," he said, his voice low and gruff. It sent tingles down her spine.

She sat up and moved away from him. "Sorry for falling asleep on you."

His eyes flashed and a low rumble sounded in his chest. "No apologies needed. I should go."

She wanted to tell him to stay, but knew that was a reckless move. She wasn't going to sleep with him tonight. God. What was she thinking? Was she really considering having sex with Zain, lord of the sexy mountain men? Yes, she was. She needed someone to make her feel alive again. But she didn't want to come off like she was desperate and pathetic. Besides, she was enjoying getting to know him.

He stood and slipped his boots on.

"I'm probably going into town tomorrow," she said to him.

"Do you need me to take you? I can pick up whatever you need if you don't want to go."

She bit her lip and stared at him. What the fuck was wrong with her? So the guy was nice. She needed to remember how to be on her own. "No, I'll do some browsing at the shops and stuff."

"If you're sure," he said. "Would you like to come over for dinner at my place?"

Was he kidding? Yes. "I don't want to bother you. I'm sure you have a ton of work." Perfect for not looking desperate or needy, but *ask me again. Ask me again. Ask me again.*

He grinned. "I still have to eat. What do you say? I can grill a mean steak."

Thank god for pushy gorgeous men. She

laughed. "Okay. I can make some sides if you want. Mashed potatoes or a salad?"

"Sounds good. Do you need me to come get you or do you think you can find your way there?" He sat on the sofa arm and watched her. Her whole body was hyperaware of his presence and the size of him.

"You said it's that one little path, right?"

"Yeah. It's only about three hundred yards. Really close."

She smiled. "All right. I'll see you tomorrow then."

He nodded and stared at her mouth for a long moment before standing and heading for the kitchen. She rushed after him.

"Zain?"

He stopped at the door, holding it open and glanced at her. "Yes?"

"You're really tall. Can you come down here for a second?" she asked.

He leaned down, bringing his face to hers.

Shit, was she really going to do this? "I just wanted to thank you for today." She should've stopped, but she couldn't. She kissed the corner of his mouth, brushing her lips over his quickly.

His eyes flashed gold again and a loud rumble sounded from his chest. "Good night, Piper."

"Good night, Zain."

God. She was going to hell. All she wanted was to keep him there and strip him slowly, peeling his clothes off like he was a gift. But she watched him go and locked the door behind him. Her heart thudded so loudly in her ears, that's all she heard.

It was going to be a difficult night, but for a totally new reason. Zain was an unexpected bonus on this strange trip. She hadn't truly wanted a man, including her ex, with such intensity. Her body was shaking from that tiny brush of her lips on his. Would she even survive a night with the big bear? She really wanted to find out.

CHAPTER SEVEN

After a fitful night of sleep, Piper got up early and sat on the covered porch with a blanket over her legs. The rain still came down while she drank coffee. She couldn't stop thinking of Zain. Or his lips. How sweet he'd been and how interesting. *Stop it. That's the last thing you need.* She sighed. It was true. She wasn't sure she was ready for dating or even considering it yet.

Zain was nice, but what did she really know about him? She snorted. What did she really know about Scott? He'd turned out to be the biggest type of asshole, and she'd been married to him for a decade. If that wasn't as shitty as it got, she wasn't sure what was.

All she knew was that the next time she got involved with any man, she'd need to at least feel wanted physically and emotionally. Scott had never even tried. She'd always accepted silly excuses for him so her own feelings wouldn't be hurt, or so her family and friends weren't aware of what a thoughtless husband he was. She'd gone as far as scheduling birthday, Valentine's, and Anniversary flowers to be sent to herself every year in his name.

She shook her head and drained her cup. Never again. If a man loved her, he'd better fucking show it. She was done allowing excuses to rule her life. And she wanted sex. The good kind. Like she wrote about. How was it that she could write all those steamy scenes but not have any in her life? Even worse, how could she write about emotions so foreign to her.

It was time for a change. She went inside and left the mug in the sink before heading upstairs to get dressed to go to town. How could she ever believe Scott was so important when she didn't even feel anything other than disappointment? Wouldn't she be more heartbroken if she loved him? *You didn't love him. You never loved him.*

That was the sad truth. Her entire marriage had

been based on her wanting to *fix* Scott. She'd wanted to make him into a success and a man that had something going for himself. It had become her sole purpose and she'd supported him because she was sure he was close to achieving that. He had.

Only thing was that he'd also realized he wasn't in love with her and decided to do something about it. *I shouldn't even be angry at him.* But she couldn't stop the hurt that burned in her chest which worried her more than anything. She wasn't the type of woman to hold grudges.

Wearing a pair of leggings, a big fluffy sweater, and a raincoat, she got into her old car and headed down the hill to the little town she'd seen on her way to the cabin. The road seemed much wider than what her yellow headlights revealed last night, but luckily, it'd stopped raining and she was now able to see clearly.

When she got to the edge of Ursuston, she took her time driving by the cute shops and stores before parking by a bookstore. The buildings were all small and looked like they came straight out of the old west. It was charming how they had wooden sidewalks.

She glanced at The Little Bookstore and

noticed a bunch of books at the front window display. One of her older books was there. She grinned and walked inside, thinking to sign whatever copies were available for them. No skin off her back—her editor would cry hearing that cliché.

"Hi, I'm Krista Little," said a petite blonde with a bright smile about Piper's own age.

"Hi, are you the owner?"

The woman smiled. "Yeah. Well, technically it belongs to my mother, but she's in Florida living the life of a snowbird while I'm here dealing with the rain at our family bookstore."

"One of my mother's favorite places to visit is Florida."

Krista nodded. "It's like once a certain age hits, they all get a calling from the motherland."

Piper giggled at the comment. "You're funny."

"Nah. What can I do for you?"

"Oh!" she gasped. "I'm sorry. I'm Piper Rain. I saw you have one of my books on your display and wanted to come in to see if you would like me to sign them for you. Maybe you can get more for them."

Krista's eyes widened. "You're Piper Rain?"

"That's me," she said. "I don't mind signing. Unless you'd rather not. I don't usually offer to do that unless I'm doing a book signing, but I was so happy to see one of my books in here."

Krista continued to stare at Piper, her jaw hanging open. "You're really Piper Rain?"

Piper fidgeted and started to feel uncomfortable. "Umm, yes."

"Oh, my god!" she squealed. "I've read all your books. ALL. OF. THEM."

"Wow, really?" Piper had met many readers who had been kind enough to read most of her books, but having written over a hundred romance novels, she didn't know many people who had read all her work.

"Even the ones you've co-written with others. You're amazing. I love all your books," Krista gushed. "I'm not going to say I'm your biggest fan, but I'm top five for sure."

"Thank you." Piper cleared her throat. "That's really sweet of you."

Krista slapped her forehead. "Of course, I'd love for you to sign some books for the readers." Krista widened her gaze again. "Oh, my gosh! Maybe we can do something better and set up a book signing." She frowned. "Unless that's inconvenient." She shook her head. "You're probably on vacation and here I am making plans for you."

"No, no!" Piper stopped her. "I'm happy to sign here. If you would like that. I'm staying up the mountain for a few weeks so it's no problem coming here for a few hours and hang out in civilization." She bit her lip. "Are you sure there are enough people who would want to have me sign to make it worthwhile?"

Krista burst into loud chuckles. "Are you kidding me? This little bookstore services at least four small towns and most of them are romance readers. You'd be surprised how many people will show up."

"If you think so. I'd be happy to."

"Thank you so much!" Krista flung her arms around Piper and hugged her before backing off quickly. "Sorry, I got excited."

She grinned, tickled that she could so easily make someone happy. "It's okay."

"Do you want to grab a cup of coffee? The café in the bakery next door makes amazing chocolate chip and oatmeal raisin cookies."

Piper glanced at Krista's genuinely cheerful face and nodded. "Sure. Why not? A cookie sounds perfect."

"Hang on a second," Krista told her. She

hurried to a set of stairs that led to the second floor and glanced up. "Vanessa! Michelle!"

A woman who appeared to be in her early thirties looked down from the top of the stairs. "Yes?"

A second came from around a rack of books on the first floor and peeked at them. Younger than the woman at the top of the stairs, they had a resemblance.

"I'm going next door to grab some coffee with Ms. Rain. Watch the shop, okay?"

The woman on the second floor frowned at them but nodded. She stared at Piper as Krista walked back to her.

The one by the bookcase stared wide eyed and nodded, her mouth hanging open.

"Let's go," Krista said and opened the front door and walked out with her. "Don't mind Vanessa—the one upstairs. She's probably your biggest fan, but she gets angry over you not doing things in your books the way she would have wanted."

Ah. Yeah. She had a lot of that type of reader. The ones who wanted her to write the story as they saw it. "No problem, I have a few of those. And the other woman? The one by the book rack?"

"Yeah, that's Michelle. She's Vanessa's younger

sister and I don't know if I'd call her or Vanessa your biggest fans, but they're both up there. Like, big time fans."

She frowned. "Wow. I don't usually meet this many people who read my work unless I'm at a book signing."

They headed into the bakery next door and immediately the scent of fresh baked cookies hit her nose and made her groan.

Krista laughed. "And that's without tasting them. Just wait."

They sat in a booth and on the table was a pretty printed menu of small plates they could order. Cool, she bet the sandwiches had the best bread. "You know what? I haven't had lunch yet. I think I'm going to have a BLT."

Krista groaned. "Damn it. I was trying to not eat, but now that you're eating, I don't need any motivation to eat." She motioned for someone behind the counter to come over. "Hey, Jessie. Get over here. We need some food."

Jessie, a tall brunette with beautiful brown eyes and a dazzling smile stopped in front of their booth. "Hey, y'all." She glanced at Piper. "Hi, I'm Jessie welcome to the café. What can I get you?"

"I'll have a BLT and a sweet tea, please."

Krista sighed. "I'll have the same. We're going to have dessert after, so no need to give me extra everything this time."

Jessie laughed and nodded. "You got it. I'll get right on that."

Once Jessie was gone, Piper glanced at her lunch companion. "This is such a cute little town. It's like something on a postcard."

Krista nodded. "I know. When my father died, I came here to live with my mom and that was my first time seeing a place like this where everyone knows each other. I mean, I'm used to big cities. My dad and I lived in Boston for a long time."

"Your parents divorced?"

Krista nodded. "You never hear of divorce with shifters, but my dad was a human that came to town on a vacation and fell in love. They tried to make it work, but my mom found her mate and that killed off any chance of them being a couple."

She frowned. "Wait. Your mom is a shifter and your dad wasn't and she left him for her mate? What is that?"

"Her mate? Like her soul mate? The one person you're born to be with. The one person to complete you."

Piper blinked. She'd been shocked to see the

guys in the forest shift into humans, and now to know they lived in a fairy tale ideology. . ."Shifters believe in that?"

Krista grinned. "Well, yeah. Because it's real."

Piper's jaw fell open. "Oh, come on. Seriously?" How could someone think the sperm and egg in their parents joined only because their lover existed.

"Yes!" Krista frowned. "All shifters believe in their fated mates. There is a person out there who is meant to be for you. It doesn't matter if you're human or shifter, it's the reality."

"But you just said your mom left your dad for her mate."

"Yeah, but she'd tried to tell him that things wouldn't work out between them. But my dad was a stubborn man. He came here and tried to buy her with expensive gifts and stuff. Mom never cared about that. They had a short lived romance. She was pregnant with me when she met her true mate. He was in town to do some work for the Alpha of the Black Peak Clan."

"How did your father take it?"

Krista shrugged. The food came and they thanked Jessie before starting to eat and going back to their conversation. "He wasn't happy. In fact, he was so unhappy, he told my mother he'd sue her for sole custody and tell the world this town was full of dangerous animals if she didn't sign papers for me to live with him."

Piper gaped at Krista while holding half her sandwich in her hands. "You're kidding!"

"Not even a little. Mom didn't want a fight and she didn't want to put Black Peak into the news in any negative way, so she signed her rights away."

"Oh, my god. So what happened then?"

Krista laughed. "I lived with my dad until I was thirteen. Then he died in a plane crash and I had no other next of kin. So I came to live with my mom."

"That's insane. Was it hard for you to be with her after all those years?"

She shook her head and took a bite of her sandwich. Piper watched her chew and took a bite of her own food, waiting to hear more. This would make a great story that wasn't romance.

"No. I knew he was hiding something because he hated talking about my mom and my stepmother always told me that if I wanted to keep the peace to never broach the subject. But when I came here and my mother told me what happened, I knew she was telling the truth." She tapped her nose. "Shifter sense. You see, I'm a shifter too."

"That's amazing."

"Nah," Krista laughed. "What about you? What are you doing here?"

Piper shrugged. "Trying to find my muse again. I just went through a shitty divorce and lost all creativity."

Krista winced. "I'm sorry. That must suck. I don't write, but I like to draw and when I'm stuck, it makes me crazy. So I can imagine how you feel."

"Thanks. I was hoping that being out here would help me calm down and stop thinking about my shitty ex and focus on starting over. Fresh start and all that."

Krista nodded. "That only works if you allow it. What are you doing way up the mountain?"

It was Piper's turn to shrug. "I'm mostly eating, drinking a shit ton of coffee and scaring the crap out of my neighbor. Poor Zain."

Krista's eyes popped wide. "Zain? Zain is your neighbor?"

"Yeah."

"How in the hell can you be bored with him to look at?"

Piper flushed and she glanced down at her food. "I don't really know him."

"Zain is the nicest guy on this mountain. He's also the alpha bear. Sexiest bear in town. What do you want to know?"

"Why isn't he married?" she asked and realized she'd been wondering that since she saw him naked in the woods.

Krista gave a wicked grin. "Because he believes in fated mates like the rest of us."

"Oh." Well, there went any thought of…of what? Zain was a freaking shifter. And he was waiting on Ms. Right Bear to fall in love. *But that doesn't stop you from being Ms. Right Now and exploring his body.* Goodness, she really had been without sex for way too long.

"Listen, Zain is not the type of guy to play with your emotions," Krista told her. "But if you have even a slight chance of getting in his pants, please take it. For every single female in this clan who hasn't gotten him to even glance her way. Do it!"

She laughed at the desperation in Krista's voice. "I thought I was bad, but you're worse."

Krista let her shoulders drop. "Meh. What can I say? I have no man. No romance and no prospects. So I'm living vicariously through your books."

She snorted. She had that thought with her characters earlier. "You and me both. That's why I'm here to try to figure out how to keep writing all those steamy books."

Krista met her gaze and grabbed her hand on the table. "You need to flush your ex out of your system, Piper. There's no better way to do that than by doing Zain. Hell, be a friend with benefits for a month. How perfect could that be? No broken hearts, no ties."

She giggled again. "You know, you're making this really hard."

"But is it working?" Krista waggled her brows.

"No." Yes, it was, but she wasn't telling her that.

Jessie returned to take their empty plates. "What can I get you for dessert?"

"Bring us some of your freshest cookies and two cups of coffee," Krista said. "Put lunch on my tab. Piper's doing a favor with a book signing at the shop, and I need her to not change her mind."

Piper shook her head but grinned at Krista. "Thanks so much for lunch, but I already told you I'd do it. I never go back on my word."

Jessie came back a few moments later with a fresh pot of coffee, mugs, and a plate of warm chocolate chip cookies.

Piper took a bite of one and gaped at Jessie. "This is so good!"

Jessie beamed. "Thank you, Piper. Enjoy, guys."

Piper watched her walk to a counter stacked with shoebox sized cardboard containers. "What are all those boxes for?"

"Jessie caters for the town too. Mainly just sandwiches and fruit. Meetings, gatherings, events at the community center. Nothing big. She doesn't need the money."

Piper glanced round the inside café area. Four other booths and four tables were full of people. "She must make a killing with these cookies. The BLT was so good and now these."

"She's the best." Krista sat up suddenly. "Oh, I think I'll order a few dozen cookies and coffee for your signing. That'd be fun."

"Oh, I'll definitely be there if there will be cookies," she joked.

"Don't worry. I've got you, girl."

They ate the cookies and drank coffee and then left the store and Krista showed her where the market to buy food was located.

"I hate to leave you, Piper," Krista sighed. "But it's Vanessa and Michelle's lunch hour and Vanessa is very bitchy if she doesn't get to eat on time."

"Thank you so much for lunch, Krista. Let me give you my cell phone so maybe you can come over and have dinner or something?" She gave Krista her phone number and waited as the book-store owner saved it on her phone then called Piper so she would save hers too.

"Or," Krista said, "you can come over to my place, but I've always wanted to go up the mountain. I bet the views up there are beautiful."

"They really are. You should come over for dinner or dessert. I'll take you to the rooftop balcony. You won't believe the beauty from there."

"I'll call you and we can set something up," Krista said and rushed off.

Piper stood on the sidewalk, looking around. The grocery building came into sight. Now would be a good time to get the things she wanted. Really what she wanted wasn't on display in the store. The display was only in the forest and in the house at the end of the path into the woods.

CHAPTER EIGHT

Piper had never been in a grocery market quite like this one. It was more the size of a gas station with a few gas pumps outside and lotto tickets inside. Fortunately, they had the items she needed.

She was busy looking at different cereal boxes when someone bumped into her.

"Oh, I'm sorry," she said, instinctively.

"No problem," said the other woman with a huff, stopping beside her.

Piper glanced to her left and saw a tall large woman glaring at her. Vanessa? The woman from the bookstore.

Piper was a curvy woman, but Vanessa was much larger and taller too. The woman was trying to intimidate her with size. Piper grabbed a box of her favorite cereal and hurried, but tried not to look hurrying, to another aisle. She was browsing the produce for fruit for her cereal when Vanessa came by her again.

"You're Piper Rain," she said. Her words sounded almost accusing.

"I am," she said, preparing for a verbal spar.

"I've read all your books." Somehow hearing the same words Krista said coming out of Vanessa's mouth didn't make her feel good.

"Thanks."

Then Michelle showed up out of nowhere, standing next to Vanessa. "I've read all your books too," she gushed, her eyes bright with enthusiasm. "I love them."

Piper smiled at Michelle. "Thank you."

"You're my idol," Michelle sighed.

"You know, you could've written some endings so differently. So much better," Vanessa told her, her voice cold and hard. "But you took the lazy way out and didn't bother developing some characters enough. You could've made some of the series *so* amazing."

Piper cleared her throat and inhaled sharply. "Thank you so much for reading my books. I really am grateful for you taking your time to do that. I know I can't please everyone with how the stories are written, but I try to stay true to my characters."

She'd memorized that response since she'd had to type it to every reader that tried to tell her how to write her books. She was the author. The stories were in her head. She couldn't read other people's minds. How could people not see that?

"You can change them," Vanessa told her. "Edit them. I can email you suggestions."

Seriously? She started walking toward the cashier. "Thank you, but I have a team of people that work on my books. They know my voice and I like how my stories came out."

"It's really great meeting you," Michelle yelled excitedly.

Piper glanced back to see Michelle smiling widely and Vanessa glaring at her. "Thank you, same."

She rushed to an empty lane to pay for her cereal, milk, and bananas before darting out of the market and going back to her car. Wow. She was on her way back to the cabin thinking about how some people would never be happy with how she wrote her books.

When she got to the cabin, she saw a note on

the kitchen table and a plate covered with foil wrap.

Piper,

I left you some lemon bars.

Yes, I baked them myself.

Don't forget dinner. Come over when you're ready tonight.

Zain

Ugh. This man was going to test her self-discipline and she didn't know how to handle it. She totally forgot to grab the stuff to make mashed potatoes. Dammit. She rummaged through the fridge and found stuff to make a salad. Not nearly as good as mashed taters. Oh, well. Salad it was. After putting it together, she took a long shower and changed into clean loungewear.

It wasn't like she was going to get laid or anything. *You could. If you tried.* No. This was just dinner. Zain was a nice guy. So why did she shave *everywhere*? Because it wasn't that she was looking to hook up, but if by some miracle things moved in that direction, the last thing she wanted was to not be prepared.

Her phone rang as she walked out of the cabin. She was surprised there was a signal.

"Hi, Mom."

"I have been waiting for your call for over twenty-four hours, young lady," her mother admonished.

She grinned and slipped one of her earbuds into her ear so she could talk without having her phone in her hand. "I'm sorry, Mom. I've been trying to relax."

"And have you?"

"I said I've been *trying*. I just got here. Give me some time."

Her mom sighed loudly. "How's the cabin?"

"It's massive. You and Aunt Sylvie could've come up and spent time here, too, and I wouldn't even notice you're here. It's that big."

"No, darling. This is you time. You need to relax and unwind. Forget all about Scott and focus on what you want for your future." She cleared her throat. "So, any good looking men up there?"

"Mom!"

"What? I'm sure there are some sexy mountain men up there that saw your beautiful face and made some dirty but much needed advances."

She chortled and almost tripped on a rock. "Mom, come on. I've only met a handful of people. The caretake seems nice."

"Oh, yes. That hunky young man I video

chatted with when I rented the cabin? Have you done the horizontal polka with him yet?"

"The what? Mom, what the hell are you talking about?"

"Did you give him some."

"No! Mom!"

"Well, you should. He was really nice, and you need to get rid of some tension. It might help you write. Even if it doesn't help you, it'll definitely be fun. You've gone too long with any."

"Is that why you called? To haggle me about my sex life which we are not discussing."

Her mom chuckled. "No, you little prude. How do you write such hot books and have this attitude? Listen, I want you to stop thinking about romance and just have fun for once in your life. When was the last time that happened?"

She shrugged, seeing the cabin up ahead. "I don't know. I've always had so many responsibilities with Scott. I haven't had fun in a long time."

"Well, that stops now. You need to take this trip and have fun. Live a little. Do something out of your comfort zone. Honey, remember how to be alive."

"I'll take your words into consideration," she said and smiled at Zain standing by the door, waiting for her. She was only a few steps away from him. "I have to go now."

"Okay, baby. Go have sex. Please. For the love of all that's creative, get your freak on! You need it!"

"Bye, Mom." She yanked the phone out of her pocket and pressed the end call button. Thank god she'd had earbuds. She'd be super embarrassed if Zain heard her.

CHAPTER NINE

Zain had a hard time holding back the growl that rose his throat at the image of fucking Piper. That was the last thing he needed to be thinking about, but her mother's words filled his head. Piper needed sex. What kind of mate was he if he didn't give her what she needed?

But he knew she wasn't the kind to just jump in bed with someone or they would've been at it last night. God knew he wanted that after he smelled her. The fact she was a human made it that much more complicated.

He would have to show her how he felt. And with her hating her ex-husband, she probably was closed off completely when it came to relationships. He blew out a breath. He had a difficult road ahead. Might as well get on and ride it with all the twists and turns coming.

As she stepped onto his porch, he reached out and took the bowl from her. "I'll take care of it," then he opened the door for her.

She glanced up at him under her long lashes. What? Was she not used to something as basic as the guy opening a door for her?

"Come on in the kitchen. You can help me with the non-grill things." On the center island, partially cut veggies waited to be finished. She picked up a knife and sliced through the cucumbers—all pieces exactly the same width, which he could never do—for the tray with ranch dressing in the center.

"Wine?" he asked. The bottle was from their own winery. The mountains were the perfect place to grow grapes. The problem was when it came to production and the old factory.

She glanced up at the bottle. "Yum. That would be great."

He pulled a couple stem glasses from the cabinet and poured the burgundy liquid into each. She dragged carrots to her and chopped off the tops and bottoms. "You know," he said, "I didn't have you come over to *prepare* dinner."

She lifted a shoulder and dropped it. Piper felt as awkward as he did. Was it because of the quasi-kiss she gave him at her place? Thinking about that, he wanted to spin her around and suck on her lips until she was breathless.

"Honestly," she said, "I haven't been on a date in over a decade. I don't know what to say or do."

He took the knife from her hand when she finished with the orange sticks. "Well, first off. . ." he took her hand and walked her to the other side of the island and lifted her to set her on a stool. She was kind of short, but that didn't bother him. Compared to his well over six-foot frame, everyone seemed short. "You sit in the guest seat and drink your wine." He placed a glass in front of her.

She smiled up at him. "Thank you."

He and his bear were ecstatic. They'd made their mate happy. Her smile was genuine, and her tension had eased away.

"Give me one minute to get the steaks. How do you like yours cooked?" She answered, then he grabbed a platter off the counter and stepped out the sliding glass door to the deck. His feet wanted to happy dance in celebration of doing something right. From what he'd heard from other males, pleasing their mates was a hard thing. They always seemed to screw it up.

He would try his hardest to be everything she needed and wanted. He had to think of her first when it came to decisions. It wouldn't be just him anymore. He'd have to get into the habit of telling her everything, so she understood what shifter culture was about. He didn't want to hide anything from her.

Meat on the dish, he closed the grill and went inside. She sat watching him, making him a bit self-conscious. Had he brushed his hair since this morning? Shit, should he have changed into slacks from his jeans? How was his breath? Why was he thinking of all this now and not before she got here? Because he was an idiot when it came to her.

When she was around, his brain particles scattered. He went from alpha cool to omega dork from just a thought about her. He set the platter on the stove.

He heard her mumble *Hemingway* to herself. First info to share was that shifters could hear a mouse from a long distance. *Ayn Rand,* she whispered next. As he pulled plates down, he glanced at her.

"How's the wine?" he asked, not thinking of anything else to say not in the category of stupid.

She flashed that smile again. "It's great. Better than what I drink at home."

"That's our best seller in the Ursus collection."

"What?" She had no idea what he was talking about.

"One of the town's biggest exports is wine."

"Oh," she sputtered, taking another drink. "It's really good. You grow grapes in the mountains?"

"Absolutely, we have loamy, gravelly soil which is perfect for growing."

"I didn't see a big winery when I drove in. Did I miss it?"

He chuckled. "Probably not. Like everything else in Ursuston, the building is small and old and not able to handle mass quantities for nationwide shipping. But they do the best with what they have."

"Why don't they build a new, bigger place?"

He shrugged, putting a piece of meat on a plate and handing it to her. "The old bears running the place don't like change, I suppose. They've done it the same way for generations."

Piper nodded. "I can understand that. Change isn't easy to handle." The scent of sadness and fear tickled his nose. Should he broach the subject with her or let it go? What was a good mate supposed to do? Shit, what would his mother have done? Where was his phone? Could cruise ships get phone calls?

He fumbled for words. "You mentioned Hemingway a minute ago. Do you normally whisper things under your breath or just testing me to see if I'm paying attention?" He smiled big to make sure she knew he was joking. Sort of.

She laughed. "No. Jeopardy is on your TV in the living room and I knew the answers to a couple questions." She spooned salad along with mac and cheese onto her plate. He hadn't expected his mate to show up in his life, so he didn't have much adult food around unless a six pack of beer, boxes of instant mac and cheese, and Cheerios counted. Then he'd be golden.

Hearing her reply, he nearly dropped his steak on the floor. "You knew a *couple* answers? That's two more than I've ever known." Not only was she beautiful, she was intelligent. Damn, he was in a boatload of trouble.

She shrugged. "Luck, I guess. I usually have no clue."

He picked up her plate and his. "You bring the glasses. We're eating out on the deck."

Her smile slipped, but she grabbed the wine and followed him through the door. "Oh," she said surprised. "You have a heater out here."

"I didn't want you to get cold, so I dug it out of the basement. Bears seldom need extra heat to stay warm. But you're human."

She smiled, warming his heart more than he thought possible. "Human, I am. Thank you."

"Sure," he replied. It wasn't like anybody else wouldn't do the same for her. He recalled her rant about her ex. Maybe the dumbass hadn't taken care of her. Good for the alpha bear. That made his screwups less bad. Hopefully.

He scooted her chair out then in, then sat across from her. "I hope you like your steak. If it's too red, we can put it back on. The grill is still hot."

She cut down into the center, clear juices giving way to pink meat. "It's perfect," she answered. "My ex always turned mine into shoe leather." She put a piece in her mouth and sexy-as-sin noises came from her. Blood rushed out of his brain, headed the other direction. He wiggled in his chair, trying to get the zipper imprinting on his cock to move.

The word *glad* croaked out of him then he cleared his throat, feeling his face heating. He must've been sitting too close to the warmer. "Glad you like it."

"You really can cook and bake," she said. "I'm impressed."

Joy flitted through him. He tried to keep from puffing his chest out and beating on it. That was a thing his dad did while the kids laughed. His father had been great with the youth in the sleuth. He could only hope to be as good. A thought about the kids tried to surface in his mind, but he pushed it back. He wanted to focus on her. And it was effortless.

They talked about simple, get-to-know-each-other things. He learned her favorite color was green. That she was a city girl with limited survival skills in the wilderness. That she seldom went anywhere, which made her a bit sad. He remembered her mother had called to make the reservation—not her.

When dinner was over, he was desperate for her not leave. He racked his brain trying to come up with a way that didn't make him sound sleazy and that he only wanted to get into her pants. But fuck, that was exactly want he'd wanted the entire meal. But it had to wait until the right time.

Hopefully, that time would be soon, or he was going to die from lack of blood to the brain.

CHAPTER TEN

At the end of dinner on the porch of her rental's owner, Piper sat amazed. The man across the table from her was like no guy in real life. He cared about what she thought, even though she was a stranger to him.

He more resembled someone she would write about. Except her main characters had flaws to make them relatable to the reader. So far, she'd yet to find one about Zain.

She was sure he wasn't perfect, but usually, she could spot those who she'd have problems with. This skill came about *after* marrying Scott, dickhead. A lot of times at book signings, fans approached her outside of the signing and wanted to ask questions or hang out. She was fine with answering stuff but drew the line on socially gathering. Too many times, highly opinionated personalities just wanted to corner her and tell her what she was doing "wrong" in her stories. People like Vanessa.

She'd gotten good at reading faces and knowing when a stranger was friendly or had an agenda. Hey, everyone was entitled to their own opinion. She just didn't want to know what it was.

Talking with Zain became easy after they sat down to eat. She relaxed from feeling so awkward and the pressure to come up with something to say. She was good at writing, but horrible at speaking. Sometimes she wished the world communicated by written language alone. That way, all had time to edit and clarify what they wanted to say instead of shit just flying out of their mouths. Her included.

She couldn't recall the last time she'd had such an enjoyable dinner with a guy. If she were still married, she'd feel like she was cheating even though it was a friendly meeting. Apparently, she was feeling more for Zain than just friendship.

He was so different from men in the city. He seemed so down to earth, so in touch with himself. He didn't feel the need to use extravagant cream to slick back his hair, or wear fancy clothes to try to prove how much money he had. He was comfortable in his own skin, which in turn, made her feel better about herself and her choices.

She stared at him across the empty glasses and crumb-filled plates. His talk about furniture joints and how to make drawers was completely over her head, but just to hear his voice made her chill. His soft aura was something she liked being next to. She wouldn't mind being next to some other parts on him either. The grin forming on her face, she had to bite back, or she'd have to explain why she was grinning about "cabinet door designs."

A cooler breeze blew against the cabin home, overpowering the heating machine by the table.

"I think it's time to go in," he said, and she helped to gather dishes to take inside to the sink. As he rinsed plates, she'd opened the dishwasher and he passed her the dish. She pulled the bottom rack out and place it between prongs. From there, she grabbed the wine glasses and set them on the top tray. By the time they were finished with the pans and bowls, the washer was neatly stacked and full.

"Wow," Zain said, standing back gawking at the

inside of the machine, "I never would've gotten all that in there. You definitely have a talent I don't."

Piper laughed. "I've been told I'm a talented writer, but never that I'm a talented dish stacker."

He smiled and slid an arm around her shoulder. "Consider putting it on your resume. I hear employers look for that kind of thing nowadays. Cross training." She couldn't help but laugh at his silliness. Her ex never made her laugh, never gave her a reason to. With Zain, she hadn't stopped smiling yet.

His hand on her shoulder was hot, penetrating her sweater top. She wondered how they would feel on her thin leggings. Maybe even under them. Zain's eyes flashed gold like he knew she was having sexy thoughts. Shifters couldn't read minds. That she was sure of, but little else.

His hand tightened as he pulled her in for a kiss. It was a slow move that let her think if she wanted this or not. Who was she kidding? Of course, she wanted this and so much more. Her lunch with Krista, the bookstore owner, came to mind.

"Zain is not the type to play with your emotions."

"But if you have a chance of getting in his pants, please take it. Do it!"

Ugh. Was she a slut if she took up the calling her gut was giving? She wasn't sure, but when he started to pull away from the kiss, she grabbed the front of his shirt and pulled him back down. So, she was a full-blown hussy. What happened on the mountain, stayed on the mountain, or some shit like that.

Their next kiss just about set her panties on fire. Their lips met, and fireworks went off in her blood. She rubbed her body over his. Whimpers rushed out of her mouth. She didn't stop to think about what they were doing, but knew something good was coming when he pulled her leggings and underwear down and off. Her sweater came next, along with her bra. She was naked in front of him and embarrassment was the last thing on her mind. The way he glanced at her body as if it were a work of art made her giddy.

"You are so beautiful, Piper. Gorgeous."

She sucked in a hard breath. Her emotions were all over the place. She shouldn't be getting her heart involved, but it was impossible. Zain was the first man to look at her like…like that. Like she was a goddess. It filled her heart with joy.

He hauled her up by her waist, seating her on the island. Her bare ass rubbed on the cool surface of the counter. He kissed her again, as if sensing her hesitation, but it was immediately stomped by the swipe of his tongue over hers. With her eyes still shut, she let his touch and the moment burrow in her heart.

She caressed his arms and chest down to the edge of his T-shirt and slid her hands up his hot body. God. He was warm and hard but smooth and she wanted to rub herself all over him.

He fluttered kisses over her chest and sucked a nipple into his mouth. Molten lava spread through her. She wandered her hands over his muscled chest. She slid a hand down his body and caressed his cock over his sweatpants.

He was hard. She gripped him a little harder. He growled, and she smiled. Who was this woman living her book fantasies? He moved away, his gaze bright gold and he licked his lips. Her heart thudded, she wanted more. She hadn't ever felt this sexual hunger in her life.

He sucked on one of her breasts, then the other, and back until she was ready to beg for him to fuck her. A soft moan left her lips. He slid down her body, licking and kissing his way between her legs. He pulled a stool and sat down, then he lifted her legs to his shoulders and lifted her ass off the counter. She lost her breath in a rush and leaned back on her elbows, watching him stare at her pussy.

He glanced up and a soft groan sounded at the back of his throat. "Seeing your pussy so slick and trimmed is making it hard to control myself. Your scent is killing me. I could eat you like the delicious dessert you are."

She swallowed and licked her lips. "Go for it."

What? Did she just encourage him? Hell fucking yes! She had never had an orgasm unless self-induced and she just knew Zain would end that sad streak. Then, as if those were the only words he needed to hear, his face dropped to her pussy so fast she squealed. She slid her fingers into his hair, gripping the strands while he fucked her with his tongue.

Piper couldn't breathe. She couldn't think. She couldn't do anything but feel. She fell back on the counter, eyes closed and body shaking with each swipe of his tongue. He shoved his face into her folds, making her whimper with every lick. He rubbed his tongue on her clit and she almost came off the counter.

The orgasm came fast and hard. Totally unexpectedly. He sucked hard on her clit one more time and she fell apart. A scream tore from her throat, her body shaking and her pussy begging to be filled.

"Zain, oh, god!"

A soft chuckle sounded from him. She glanced down, still trying to catch her breath and met his gaze. He was licking his freaking lips.

"You make a great appetizer," he said and helped her sit up. "Now, time for the entrée."

Yes! Fuck, yes! She was ready to throw herself at him when the doorbell rang.

He grinned and winked. "Guess we'll have to wait a while."

She wanted to stomp her feet and demand to be fucked then and there, but that would make her look like a desperate woman. And as much as she wanted to get into his pants, she had some dignity. Okay, she didn't, but she didn't want to seem pathetic either. She'd wait. Even if it killed her.

CHAPTER ELEVEN

"Alpha, we're here." A young voice rang through Zain's home.

Fuck! He'd forgotten about the clan kids coming over to play video games tonight. But he had to admit, he had a superb excuse for forgetting.

His mate tasted so. Good enough to tell the teens to go home. He growled deeply and helped Piper, who was in a small panic, down from the granite island.

"Oh shit. Shit, shit, shit," Piper chanted quietly as she struggled to get dressed. "Did you neglect to tell me you had people coming over?"

He knew he was in the wrong here but

watching his little mate scramble like the hounds of hell were after her was endearing.

"Be there in just a minute," he replied. "Go ahead and get the system set up." As far as he was concerned, he wanted everyone in the sleuth to know who she was to him. He'd finally found his mate. She walked into his life on a chance of her mother seeing his ad for renting.

"Sorry, babe. I was a bit distracted."

Piper froze, bent over grabbing her pants, and gave him the evil eye. He covered his grin. She was so damn cute.

"You don't look too sorry." She mumbled under her breath. Something about dumbass men and her luck. With a huff, she stood and slapped her hands on her hips, frown on her face. "Something like this is totally going into my next book."

Another burst of laughed bubbled up in him. He tried to swallow it, but it came out through his lips sounding like a motorboat. She smiled. "This is too golden not to use."

"Glad to be of help," he replied. "If you're interested, I got some other great ideas I can show you while you're here."

Her eyes widened as her hand slapped over her mouth. "You did not just say that. Oh my god."

He was confused why her reaction was so. . .excited? "You want to be friends with benefits with me?" She whispered the last words. Hopefully, the kids were too involved in games to listen to them.

Friends with benefits? What did that mean? How could he ask her what she was talking about and not sound like an idiot? Fake it. "Absolutely, that is if you want that," he answered.

She stared at him, sucking on her bottom lip. Her eyes shined with happiness. Piper was quiet to the point he thought he'd said something stupid. "Walk me home?"

"Sure." He didn't want the night with her to end.

"Let me go to the bathroom for a moment first." He gave her directions and she hurried out. This was his chance. He rushed into the other room where the teens were already playing games.

"Hey, Rubia," he whispered, "what does friends with benefits mean?"

The girl's jaw dropped. "Are you serious? You don't know what that is?"

He rolled his eyes. "Forgive me for being an adult."

She giggled and answered. "Is she your mate?"

He could play dumb and say no, but she probably figured he was an old geezer anyway.

"Yes, but don't tell anyone yet. She doesn't know. She's human."

All the kids groaned and turned to him. "Good luck with that," one of the boys said. Why would Spud say that? His father was human. Did the teen know something he didn't?

"What do you mean?" he asked the boy.

"My mom says my dad was impossible when it came to our culture."

Rubia turned to him. "Don't pay attention to that. That's a guy thing. Girls are much easier to work with. They get it."

Get what? Goddess, he felt stupid. And he thought he'd been good at keeping up with the youth.

Sally leaned back on the bean bag, game controller in her hand. "So you're not *friends* any more with that female in town?"

What female? Piper stepped into the room with her beautiful smile. He cleared his throat. "Hey, guys, I'd like you to meet Piper Rain. She's renting the old alpha cabin for the month."

The youths turned their focus from the TV to his mate and mumbled greetings. He grabbed her hand and rushed her out the front door before someone said something he'd have to explain.

Before he got the door closed, one of his teens hollered, "Don't worry, Alpha. We'll lock up."

Piper glanced at him. "What does that mean?"

"Nothing. Just something we were talking about." He needed to change the subject fast. "That was a great salad you made." His bear grumbled that he was a moron.

"Thank you," she said then laughed. "I think the steak was much better than the lettuce, tomatoes, and ranch dressing."

He shuffled his feet, excited that she liked his cooking. He would always be able to feed her, in human and bear forms.

"It's just a guy thing." He started. "It's just slap it on, flip it over—"

"Set it on fire and then it's done," she finished for him with a laugh.

Wow, she was paying attention earlier. Not that he thought she wasn't. . .He squeezed her hand, loving the feel of it in his.

The moonlight streamed down in patches through the leaves, lighting her beautiful face. He could sit and look at her forever.

"So," she said, "you have kids over a lot?"

Safe question. "I do. It's important to me to keep up with the younger generations. The world changes so fast. So many of the kids go to school and don't come back. If I get behind, our clan could be left vulnerable or dwindle to nothing."

"Kinda like the town?" she asked. "All the buildings are old. And like you said about the winery, change would be too much for them."

"Yeah, the town is a great example. It's slowly dying." Something needed to happen to reinvigorate the owners, bring in consumers and money. But besides taking out massive loans to rebuild, he didn't know what they could do.

All that worry was for another time. Right now, his mate was his focus. He had to find a way of getting her to fall in love with him so she'd stay. Maybe accepting her strange request for being *friends* would be a way to her heart.

Now, how did he bring that up without sounding like a huge perv? Goddess, help him.

CHAPTER TWELVE

Hiding in Zain's guest bathroom, Piper took a deep breath then let it out. Just like the bookstore owner said, Zain wanted to be a benefit friend. Her pulse pounded in her ears. Was this something she could do? She'd never had casual sex before. Her heart had always been part of the act.

She closed the toilet lid and sat, dropping her head into her hands. God knew she wanted to say yes. Not only because she hadn't had sex in years, not to mention no orgasms for longer, but she hadn't had the comfort of loving arms holding her, no kisses, no snuggling, no person-to-person contact. The basic human needs to survive.

Standing, she paced between the pedestal sink

and two-person, walk-in shower, which was freaking gorgeous all decked out in tile to the ceiling. Speaking of which, Scott never had sex with her in the shower. Granted their tub/shower combo wasn't conducive to that activity, but the point was he never tried.

But what did her heart say about the matter? Besides her second encounter with Zain where she almost stabbed him with a butcher knife, she'd felt safe and comfortable. She didn't have to walk on eggshells around him—damn, another cliché—like she had with Scott for years. Not to mention that looking at his body got her heart racing—her heart was definitely playing a role.

Shit, if she stayed in here much longer, they would think she was taking a dump. Going number two in a virtual stranger's home was so not the thing to do. She took another deep breath, letting it out slowly. She could do this.

With a smile, she left the small room and saw Zain in the living room with the kids. That was interesting. She wouldn't have thought the alpha of a town would take the time to give attention to the young. Maybe there was more to him than first appeared.

She didn't remember much of the walk to

Zain's mother's home after discussing the kids. Her brain was spinning with what to do. She needed to stay calm or she'd throw up on his shoes. Would he accept an invite for sex after she barfed the wonderful dinner they ate?

As they approached the door, he slowed, and she wondered if he'd changed his mind. Well, tough for him. She'd made the decision and her heart agreed. She tugged on his hand, pulling him through the front door and up the stairs. When they reached the bedroom, Zain put the brakes on.

"Whoa, here," he said, surprising her, making her stop her crusade to get him into bed. He took his phone out of his pocket, and a moment later, soft music played through the room.

"How did you do that?" she asked. The music calmed her nerves and relaxed her stress.

He walked her to the balcony doors then set his phone on a small table. "Bluetooth. The house is set up with speakers in all the rooms." He opened the French doors leading onto a private balcony. Did he want to have sex where the whole world could see?

Before she knew what he had in mind, he twirled her into his arms, one hand settling on her lower back, the other holding hers over his heart.

He pulled her against him, and her body went crazy with want. They swayed to the music.

His chest and abs were solid, but nothing felt as hard as his cock pressed against her lower stomach. Well, at least they were on the same page. And he didn't want to do it out in nature. She didn't think.

"This is better," he said with a smile, gazing at her. They rocked side to side putting her into a hypnotic lull, under his spell. "You are so beautiful. I can't help but stare at you sometimes."

Her face heated. She hadn't heard words like those in a long time. Her confidence level rose. He thought she was pretty. His laugh rang out at her shyness. She laid her head against his chest. He felt like a tree. Solid and strong. A slight vibration buzzed through his body to hers. Sounded like a cat purring. Wasn't he a bear?

Snuggled against him, she'd never been so content. He was warm and she felt safe in his arms. The rain-cleaned air invigorated her body, giving a boost in spirit.

"Are you enjoying your vacation?"

She pulled back to look up at him. "It's not really a vacation. I'm supposed to be writing."

"You just got here. You have weeks. Relax and

enjoy the area for a while. You know, they say that city folk are out of touch with nature, making them off balance."

"I'd heard something like that. I read that being in nature can lower blood pressure and stress hormone levels. Probably reduces anxiety and helps with a better mood. I remember a research finding that being in nature calms as well as eases feelings of isolation—"

Zain's laughter rang out again.

"What?" she said.

"I was thinking along the lines of hiking, not medically studied research. You're way too smart for this mountain bear."

"No, I only know that because I had a story about a woman who went from city dwelling to living in a rural area," she replied. "I'm not that smart. I just know a lot of trivia that is useless unless you're on Jeopardy."

He laughed. "And you're funny. How can you be more perfect?"

His words blew away the thoughts she had. Did he really mean that or was it just words to get her into bed? What the hell was she thinking? That was her goal too.

His eyes melted darker. "Is that disbelief, I

smell?" He lowered his head, his lips meeting hers in a rush of suppressed passion. The kiss was deep and sure. It lit a fire in her belly. Before she knew it, she was in his arms, being carried into the bedroom.

Then he deposited her on the bed and met her gaze. His glittering eyes focused on her chest, until her nipples tightened, and flames crowded her cheeks.

"I want you, Piper," he told her, his voice deep and rough.

"I-I want you too."

Get it together, Piper. This is what you've been wanting. No time for nerves now. He kissed her again, making her forget all about nerves or feelings of awkwardness. Then her clothes were off, and she was panting for breath, her eyes trained on his body.

"You still have clothes on."

He grinned. "Do I hear a little bossiness?"

She raised her brows. "Get them off. Now."

A chuckle sounded from him and then his clothes were gone. He caressed his hands up her thighs. His hands were warm, rough. They looked huge sliding up her thighs.

"I can't wait to taste you again." His voice was a

low rumble that heated her from the inside. He lowered on the bed, pushing her legs apart, his face only inches from her sex.

"Good god," she gasped, her body flaming in need.

He grinned and winked, "Relax. It won't hurt."

When he shoved his face into her pussy, she almost came off the bed. The man was a beast and she was ready to beg him to eat her up. God, she was so easy. He swiped his tongue up and down her sex, flicking and probing and making her gasp and squirm. She flung herself back on the bed, her hands immediately gripping his hair and her ass coming off the bed to push her pussy closer to his mouth. He was going to make her come and she was going to let him.

Piper moaned. He growled, his loud vibrations sent shivers down her spine. He held her wide open, licking her repeatedly. And boy was he liking it. He groaned with every lick. He made her feel like a decadent dessert.

His face came up from her pussy, coated in her honey and she groaned. "You're like a delicious dessert." He licked again. "I can eat you all night. I can't wait to taste your come on my tongue again."

She moaned again, her body shaking from her need to come. "Zain…"

He rolled his tongue over her clit and then met her gaze. "Yes, beautiful?"

"Please, make me come."

He flattened his tongue against her pussy and flicked it in and out of her channel, making her whimper and her legs shake.

"Oh, god."

He licked, sucked, and nibbled. As if that wasn't enough to make her lose her mind, he growled softly, fucking her with his tongue then running it over her clit like a one of her battery operated toys.

She tensed, her body tight as she fell into her climax. She screamed, her body shaking with the force of her orgasm. A wave of bliss swept her under. He continued licking her, sucking her folds and dragging mini explosions from her body.

She huffed and tried to catch her breath, her body shaking and electric currents running down to her pussy. He really was gifted. She'd thought for sure that first time had been a mistake from her lack of sex, but no. Zain was the first and only man to give her orgasms and epic ones at that.

"I want inside you," he said, his voice a low rumble. "Do you want me, Piper?"

Hell yes! She nodded quickly. "I'm all yours."

He grabbed her legs and pulled down, dragging her to the edge of the bed. He pushed her legs wide and drove deep in one harsh drive. She moaned at the thick, full feeling. With his hands curled around her waist, lifted her into his arms, and switched positions. He sat with her riding his cock and cupped her face in his hands.

She hadn't been this close to his face before. Her pussy fluttered around his cock. He kissed the valley of her breasts, licking his way up to her jaw. "You are mine, beautiful. All mine."

She needed this. Him. A man that truly wanted her and could give her the pleasure she'd been denying herself for too long. His hands caressed her bare arms and went back around her waist.

He swooped down and latched on to her lips at the same time he lifted her and dropped her over his cock, taking her lips and her sex as his. It was too much. Her body jerked at the invasion.

She whimpered into the kiss, sucking on his tongue and letting him into her mouth, letting him fondle her lips, and then following it back to his so she could do the same to him.

She tore from the kiss, the lack of oxygen making her lightheaded. Her pussy felt aflame as he lifted and dropped her so fast on his cock she swore they'd catch fire.

He pressed her down hard, rubbing her clit on his pelvis and locked gazes with her. "So perfect. Did you know that? You're beautiful and perfect, Piper."

She swallowed at the dryness in her throat. A soft groan left her lips, her pelvic muscles squeezing at his hard length. "Thank you."

"Don't thank me," he grunted, another drop and rocking her over his pelvis, rubbing her clit against him. "I speak the truth. You're beautiful all over."

She arched her chest into him, pressing herself tightly against him. Her nails dug into the back of his neck as he continued bouncing her up and down and rocking her until every inch of his cock was deeply inside her. He kissed her hard and deep, making her forget everything but the feel of his body invading hers.

She kissed him, secretly allowing love to touch her heart for the first time in her life. Zain was making her want more than she ever dreamed possible. The tension building escaped her reach. She jerked as his movements increased in speed and harshness.

Then she tensed as the orgasm shook her to the

core. She held on to him, riding the wave of pure bliss. Her pussy grasped at his hot length. The tension at her core unraveled with the continued onslaught of mini-explosions taking over her system. The string of orgasms left her breathless and shaking.

He grunted and pressed her down, pushing his cock as deep as possible as he came in her. His hot cum filled her channel.

They laid on the bed, catching their breaths, her body half splayed over his. He had a hand possessively over her ass and the other caressing her back. He kissed the top of her head and pulled her even closer. A sense of belonging filled her. Her emotions were all over the place. Her heart told her Zain was the man she'd been waiting for. But her brain told her to chill and keep it sexual. Emotions were messy. She needed to keep her head on straight.

"I love holding you," he said softly and continued to caress her spine.

Her heart was in trouble. Big trouble.

CHAPTER THIRTEEN

Piper smiled as she drove down the curvy mountainside road, the early afternoon sun peeking through the trees. Thinking back to last night, she'd never experienced anything so intimate, so loving, so mind blowing. Now she understood what those sex scenes in her stories were about.

Yes, she had the words and actions and a well-used Kama Sutra with pictures in her office. Otherwise, she wouldn't have been able to pull off being a romance author for years. But the real emotions and physical feelings were foreign to her. No longer. She wondered if she would be able to write now.

But first, she needed to drop by the bookstore

to go over general plans for the book signing. She wanted simple and local. The last thing they needed was hundreds of people from halfway across the country cramming into the town. Cars would be parked *everywhere*. There was only the one main street through the old town and no parking lots to hold over a few cars. Ugh. She didn't want to think about that mess. Simple and local.

When she reached the door, a bright yellow flyer taped to the glass portion flashed her name across the top with "Ask an Author." That was kind of catchy. Answering questions was much easier than coming up with stuff to talk about.

Stepping inside, she smelled the scents of old leather and papers, relaxing her worries. Nothing was as soothing. A few shoppers grazed the shelves, occasionally picking up a book and reading the back cover. She dreaded writing the back blurb. She could put seventy thousand words on paper but had a hard time writing fifty.

She took her time walking through the store looking for the owner, Krista, if she remembered correctly. After the incredible sex last night, she wasn't sure how many brain cells she had left. They'd all burst during her third orgasm or was it the fourth? A chill ran through her and she wiggled with happiness and excitement. They hadn't made plans before Zain went to work this morning. But he had her number.

"Piper!" She turned toward the voice to find the owner and Michelle shelving books. Piper hurried over and gave both a quick hug. "What do you think of the flyer?" Krista's face beamed with delight.

"It's eye catching, definitely. How many have you sent out," *already*? she thought.

"Just the locals and the town over yonder where a lot of my clientele come from."

That didn't sound too bad. "Great. I didn't want to make this a big deal and put a lot of pressure on you."

Krista waved her comment away. "Don't worry about that. The bakery next door is making some snacks and drinks, the community center is letting us borrow chairs, my friend is setting up the sound system, and your latest book we ordered by the box to be here the day before."

Well, she made that shit look easy.

The owner leaned closer and whispered to her, "You know, someone is bound to ask about all the sex you write."

Yeah, that topic always came up. No one believed she used resources to write the hot stuff. So just like in her book, she made up a story for the audience's satisfaction. But now, damn, she did have experience to draw upon. Boy, did she ever. Shit. There was no way she was using anything from last night. Zain would just die if all the women in the sleuth knew they slept together.

Krista sniffed. "Hmmm. Anything you want to talk about?"

Piper froze. *Oh shit.* "What do you mean?"

Krista looked around. No one was nearby except Michelle who looked as interested as her boss did.

"Girl," Krista said, "we're shifters. We can smell everything. Even emotions. And you are pumped for sex."

Her jaw dropped. "Seriously?" Thinking of what she was thinking about, her face turned very hot. She slapped her cool hands on her burning cheeks. "Oh my god." But they couldn't possibly know who she did the deed with, thank god.

"Glad you took my advice. So, how good is the alpha in bed?" Krista whispered. "I've heard he's an animal."

Michelle groaned. "Krista, that joke is so old."

The owner frowned. "Well, it's what you said first."

Michelle turned back to Piper. "Well?"

Piper, for the first time in a long time, had nothing to say. Her mouth opened and closed with no words coming out. How did she tell them without telling them? "Uh, we're FWB," she said.

Krista's eyes bugged out, she gaped and slapped her hands on Piper's shoulders. "You're so damn lucky. You have to tell us *everything.*"

Oh god. The woman couldn't be serious. She wasn't telling anybody anything. Piper winked. "If you want to know, then you need to read my next book."

Krista squealed and bounced on the balls of her feet. "I can't wait. When will it be out?"

"I haven't written it yet." Piper tried to calm the woman. She was drawing unwanted attention.

Michelle glanced at her watch. "Krista, it's time for me to take the snacks to the community center."

"Oh," the boss pushed the girl toward the door, "get going. Don't make those boys wait."

When Piper realized that Michelle was leaving, she asked to tag along just to get out.

"That'd be great." Michelle led her out the front

door and through the entrance to the café/bakery. "Hey, Jessie," Michelle hollered at the empty counter, "we're here for the stuff to take to the boys' meeting."

"Coming," Piper heard in the hall to the counter from the kitchen. Around the corner, the female who served them yesterday carried a box and set it next the cash register beside an identical box. Inside were the shoebox-sized containers for catering.

"Hey, Piper, good to see you again," the bakery owner said. "You helping Michelle today?"

"Yeah," Michelle said, lifting a box. "This way you don't have to lock up the bakery to leave."

"Well, I appreciate that a lot." Jessie gave them a bright smile. Piper grabbed the second container and followed her new friend. She backed out the door and caught up to her companion on the cracked sidewalk. She had to watch where she was walking so her toe wouldn't trip on the uneven path.

"So, where are we going?" she asked.

"Every Friday afternoon after school lets out, Zain and several of the kids get together to have a meeting of the Explorers Unit."

"What's that?"

"It's a national group with adults and kids who do community projects and team building stuff. They've cleaned up along the side of the highway, painted one of our elder's home. That kind of thing."

"Wow," she said, "that's really cool."

Michelle shrugged a shoulder. "Keeps everyone out of trouble on a Friday night. It's hard to justify cruising the three blocks through town then turn around and go back."

Piper laughed. "I can just imagine all the cars lined up out here."

Michelle snorted. "Yeah, that's all we need." She repositioned the box in her arms and stopped to open a full glass door with another of the flyers advertising her Ask an Author. A cacophony of voices and music met her in the entrance.

"Food's here," she heard, and the box disappeared from her hands so quickly, she wondered if she'd dropped it. Two older teens had the containers, walking toward several long tables in the main room.

Michelle continued toward the kids who unpacked the small containers then demolished whatever was inside. Piper recognized several faces from Zain's video game session last night.

Her face heated. Those kids knew Zain hadn't come back to the house after walking her to her place. They had to think she and Zain hooked up. Please, don't let anyone say anything.

A door to the side opened and Zain walked out with papers in his hands. He immediately stopped and sniffed the air. Oh shit. Could he smell the same thing the bookstore owner did? Oh god, how embarrassing.

Michelle hurried toward him and looked like she was going to shake hands or greet him somehow. Zain's eyes landed on her, though, still by the front door. They turned liquid gold. His animal. She gasped. Seeing that really struck her as sexy. But here was definitely not the place for that.

He avoided Michelle's arms, patting her on the shoulder, mumbled something, but never took his eyes off her. With a few strides, he had reached her, his arms going around her. He buried his nose in her hair and breathed deeply. His chest vibrated like he was purring again. That was so cute.

"I'm glad you're here, but why?" he said, still squeezing her to him.

She grinned and let him hold her longer than what was probably socially acceptable. "I helped Michelle bring over snacks." She pushed on him a tiny bit, so he'd step back. Her eyes rolled toward the group which had stopped eating and stared at them. "Umm, the others are looking at us." She tried to control the blush but failed big time.

The gorgeous alpha smiled. "Don't worry about them. Half of them figured it out already. They locked up the house and I still wasn't back."

"Yeah," she raised her voice a tad, "that was a nice long walk we had last night."

The girls giggled. "Oh god," Piper moaned, dropping her head onto his chest. He took her hand and pulled her to the tables.

One of the boys smirked to the others. "Yeah, I bet it was long. And thick too." As she and Zain passed behind the kid with the smart ass comment, Zain playfully smacked the back of the kid's head, flopping the long hair into the young face.

"Shut it, Spud, before I put you on latrine duty."

"Aww, come on, Alpha," he whined, "nobody ever uses them."

Zain gave him a half serious face. "Lucky for you then."

At the end of the long table, he put her next to him as he stood and knocked a gavel on the plastic. "I call this Meeting of Unit Explorers to order."

All the kids quieted and looked at him. Wow,

she'd never seen kids snap to attention like they had.

"Sally, run roll call please," he said. Each of the fifteen kids raised a hand as present.

Zain passed around the papers he had in his hands when he came out the door. "Look over the minutes from the last meeting. Any corrections?"

Piper studied the page, saw some grammatical errors and a few not-so-good word choices, and a misspelled word.

"Any corrections?" the alpha called. Nobody said anything. She just smiled. That was one reason she loved her editor. Most people didn't catch shit like that.

One of the boys called out, "I make a motion to approve the minutes as written."

A girl spoke up right after him. "I second that motion."

Damn, Piper was impressed. She'd never been to a meeting that was held in such an official manner. And here Zain was teaching them. She would've loved to have had something like this during school. They carried out motions down the agenda to get to *Old business: river rafting*. What did that mean?

Spud popped up from his chair. "I make a

motion that we keep the date for the annual river raft as tomorrow." Getting a good look at him, she noted he looked like a professional football player. Damn, they grew them big here.

Several "seconds" rushed out.

Zain leaned forward, putting his hands on the table. "I don't know, guys. The weather—"

"Please, Alpha," one of the girls said. "It hasn't rained all day."

"No, Rubia," he replied, "but it has the past five days and is forecasted for tomorrow."

"We just leave early before the front comes through."

"Yeah, Fen's right," Spud said. "Rain isn't scheduled until the afternoon."

Zain stood back, crossing his arms over his chest, staring down at the table. Piper could feel the tension in the room. Every teen was on the edge of their seat, literally, staring as Zain pondered his decision.

"Sounds pretty cool to me." Why Piper said that, she wasn't sure. She'd never been but had googled the topic once to get the words and basics to write a scene.

Zain raised a brow at her. "You want to come?"

Oh shit. All eyes fixated on her. She swallowed hard. "What happens if I say yes?"

"We go," Zain replied.

"And if I say no?"

Groans and moans erupted around the table. Zain shushed them. "Don't put any pressure on Piper."

She whispered to herself, "Too late for that."

The group laughed. Dammit. She forgot they had super hearing. She took a deep breath and held it for a moment. It would be great experience for another scene. She did know how to swim, so... "Why the hell not. Let's go."

Cheers rang out from the teens. Zain raised both brows at her. She shrugged. "What the hell? The worst that can happen is I drown."

CHAPTER FOURTEEN

*Z*ain stood at the head of the meeting table, really not liking what his mate just said. He leaned over and snatched her from her chair into a tight hug. His animal clawed at his skin, not happy either. She would not die. He would protect her always.

After a moment, she said, "Zain, I was joking." He didn't let her go. The kids had quieted. "Zain, the children are watching us."

"That's fine," he growled. "They need to learn how to take care of their mate." Fuck. Had he just called her his mate out loud? Hopefully, she didn't catch it. He put her back in the chair. "Okay, what else is there?"

The meeting continued, but he barely heard

what was said. His mind was on his mate and the danger she could be in. He hadn't thought about that when he made the dumbass move to ask her to go. He really thought she would decline and make it an easy decision. Nope, not his mate. He couldn't hide his grin.

He adjourned the meeting and told the group to pull out everything they needed for tomorrow's adventure. A boy opened a narrow door to a storage room and the teens packed in, soon carrying out paddles, lifejackets, and stuff.

Zain pulled up a chair beside his mate, took her hand and pulled her onto his lap. He breathed her in. Damn, so good.

"Zain," she tried to stand, "what are you doing? There are kids here."

"And, as I mentioned, they need to learn how to treat their mates. They'll be at this stage soon." He was serious when he said that.

Her eyes narrowed on him. "What do you mean by mate?" Zain was up and out of the chair so quickly, his head spun.

"Hold on, Fen," he said, hurrying toward the storage room, "let me help you." He was going to kick himself for saying that word again. But dammit, that's what she was. They'd needed to have long talk after this. He disappeared into the closet and leaned against the wall where no one outside could see him.

"Alpha?" Val said, "You okay?"

He plopped a hand on the boy's shoulder. "Yeah. Don't worry about me. One of these days, you'll understand."

"Only if his mate is a human," Spud mumbled on his way out the door. That boy seemed to know a lot more than he did when he was that age. But that was a long damn time ago too. Keeping up with the newer generations left him speechless at times. He unrolled the air compressor line and stretched it into the room where the rafts had been laid out.

He noticed his mate talking with a couple of the girls. He didn't want to be nosy, but dammit, he was. No telling what they would tell her about shifters. So he listened in occasionally, you know, just to make sure whatever they said was correct.

Piper asked, "Is that normal for him, to just wig out?" He guessed she was talking about him.

The girls giggled. Rubia replied, "Only with you, I think." He froze in his crouched position. That conversation headed quickly where he wished it would not go.

"Why only me?" Piper said.

The two kids looked at each other and smiled. Shit. Should he get up to interrupt? He didn't want her run off screaming thinking something horrible.

"Wait, I got it." Piper said. "It's a shifter thing."

The ladies gasped and eyes went wide. "You know about shifters?" Sally whispered.

"Not really," she answered. "I know of them and I know they can see in the dark and smell just about any damn thing. What else can they do?" Piper stepped closer to the girls.

Oh, shit. This was getting serious now. Rubia sucked in her bottom lip, eyes catching his. He gave her a slight shake of the head. Now wasn't the time for his mate to know things she didn't understand fully.

"Well," Rubia said, "shifters are really fast and strong." Piper nodded. "We can hear things from a long ways away."

"And when we find our mate, our animal knows right away. We don't have to date like humans do. Unless we want to," Sally added. Rubia slapped her arm, glanced at him and murmured in her friend's ear. Sally's eyes good big, looking at him. He gave her an expression of calmness. It was fine as long as they didn't go any further with that discussion.

"So a mate is a girlfriend or boyfriend?" Piper asked.

The girls looked at each other again, eyes wide, then turned to her and both said, "Yes."

He cringed and stared down at the raft he was supposedly inflating. Shit. Now what was he going to say. Would she flip out if she thought they were playing house for a bit? He wasn't going to play long. It would become real rather damn quickly if he had his way.

"Hey, Alpha," Spud smiled at him. "I see you're having problems airing that up. Would you like me to help you?" From his crouched position, Zain slowly looked up at the kid just out of his reach. Smart. Spud busted out with a laugh, slapping his thigh, and hooting.

"Double latrine time," Zain hollered, not holding back his smile.

Spud froze, his smile flipping over. "What? Come on, Alpha. You know I'm not serious."

Fen walked by and slapped Spud on the arm. "Lucky. I'd gladly do latrine time."

Spud called after her. "No, you wouldn't. It sucks rocks."

Zain gave him a disapproving look.

"Sorry, Alpha. I know you don't like us saying things like that. But it's true."

"Here," Zain handed him the air line, "blow up all the rafts and stack them for tomorrow. I'm depending on you to get this all set up. Understand?"

The student snapped up straight, saluting. "Aye, aye, Captain. I'm your man for blowing up shit." A toothy grin popped onto the young face.

Zain could only shake his head and walk away. Though most of the boys were big for their age because they were shifters, Spud—he got his name from eating an entire bushel of mashed potatoes when he was younger—was bigger and stronger than most. He was the one Zain went to when he needed help with the younger generations. The boy was a born alpha, very smart, and very smart ass.

He headed toward his mate and the two girls. Time to grab all her attention before the girls said something *he* would regret.

"Hey, ladies," he greeted. Piper's expression was one of happy surprise. "What?" he asked. Had he missed something important in their conversation?

She shook her head. "Nothing. You just called us *ladies*."

"Yeah," he said slowly, "that's what you are."

She waved away the conversation. "Never mind. Most men would've referred to us as *girls*."

"Ahh, got it," he said even though he didn't. He took her hand and led her toward the tables. He leaned against one and pulled her in front of him, her back to his chest, arms around her waist. He wasn't sure what to say.

She twisted around to look up at him. "This is a really cool thing to do with the kids. How long have you been meeting?"

"We've done this the past five years or so," he answered. "I wanted to find ways to keep in touch and came across this organization that teaches kids different things they can use throughout their lives. It's been good on both sides."

He pulled his phone out and held it in front of her while he typed in the URL for the weather. The forecast popped up.

"You think it's too bad to go tomorrow?" she asked.

He sighed. "I don't know. We've had a lot of rain, but it's not rained today, so it will probably be fine. Are you sure you want to go?"

"Yeah," she replied. "It will be fun. I don't have a clue how to paddle or anything, but I'm a fast learner."

"Oh, no," he shot back, "you are *not* sitting on the outside. You will be in the middle seat where your only responsibility will be to hold on." He smelled a light scent of anger, but he wasn't putting her in any danger. He had a mind to cancel tomorrow just so there was no opportunity for anything to go wrong.

"Fine," she said, "just don't disappoint the kids by telling them we're not going. Did you see the excitement on their faces when the topic came up? You would've thought it was Christmas."

He chuckled as he swiped on his phone for the hourly rain prognosis for tonight and tomorrow. The boys were right. It wasn't supposed to rain for another twenty-four hours. Looked like he didn't have a reason to say no. He slid his phone back into his pocket and hugged her close to him, kissing the top of her head. Her hair smelled so good.

He leaned down to her ear and whispered, "How are you today after last night?" He tried not to smile when he scented her shyness and embarrassment. This woman wrote erotic sex scenes for a living, yet she was so bashful in real life. How strange.

"How do you think?" she whispered back. "I could barely walk this morning." Being a shifter, he was thicker than human males, but he didn't think he would injure her. A virgin he could understand being sore, but a married woman shouldn't have been that way.

His hold on her grew tighter with his concern. "Did I hurt you?" His heart pained with the thought of his selfish actions. He'd promise to never touch her again if that was what she wanted.

She turned in his arms to face him. "Zain, stop freaking out. That's normal for someone in my situation."

His brows pulled down. "What do you mean? What situation?"

She waved her hand, brushing away his question. "Never mind. Not important. Are we doing anything tonight?" she whispered.

Excitement raced through him, but he had to shut it down with their younger audience. "How about I come to your place after this is over? Shouldn't be much longer. Just need to line everything up for the morning."

"Perfect. I'll get going, then. Need to make sure

everything is ready for you." Her devilish smile sent blood rushing far south.

"You can't leave now," he replied and rubbed his rock hard dick against her. "What would the kids think if they saw that?"

She grinned and patted his chest. "I'm sure you can come up with something." She pulled out of his arms. "Oh, should I take those boxes back to the bakery?"

"Nah. I think Michelle comes back later to get them," he said.

She leaned over and pulled out two plastic containers remaining in the box. "We can munch on these until we eat." She winked and walked out, shaking that ass in a delicious way.

CHAPTER FIFTEEN

Piper squirmed in the driver's seat. She couldn't wait for Zain to get to her place. They'd have hours together. She'd be way sorer tomorrow. He'd have to carry her anywhere they'd go.

She slowly made the last hairpin curve that led to the driveway up to the cabin before continuing to the bridge over the small river. When she applied brakes to turn, from the corner of her eye, she saw a flash of yellow in the trees. Piper pulled onto the gravel drive then stopped.

Staring out the side window, she searched for something that should've stood out like a sore pinky finger. *Thumb* would've been a bad cliché.

Several yards in, from behind a tree, a small face leaned into view. The little girl she met in the woods.

Piper jumped out of her car. "Emma?" When she stepped into the woods, the girl ran. Piper took off after her. "Emma, wait. I just want to talk to you. Emma." Piper ducked under low branches and hopped over tree roots at high speed. Ugh. This was so not her thing. Almost out of breath, she hollered, "Emma, come talk to me. I have food."

The girl stopped and turned. Piper finally reached her and kept the gasp to herself. The child was dirty like she'd been rolling on the ground. Her jeans had holes and her shoes were on the wrong feet. If she could see the shirt under the bright raincoat, would it be as torn and dirty?

"Looks like you've been playing hard. You've got a little dirt on you face." She smiled to let the child know she was being funny. The young one lifted a hand to her face and Piper saw dirt packed under her fingernails. "Girl, you need a bath."

Emma stepped back. "No. The water is too cold."

"You need to turn the hot on more."

The girl shook her head. "There is no hot water. Only the stream. Can I have some food?"

"Sure, it's in my car." She held a hand out to the girl. "You want to come with me?" Emma slid her little hand into Piper's. She wondered what the child meant by the stream. What stream? Surely her home had a hot water heater.

Piper opened the passenger's door and picked up the container that had half a sandwich. Then she looked at the girl's filthy hands. No way was the child eating with those.

"Tell you what," she said, "we need to wash your hands. So how about you come to my house, we'll wash them, then you can eat."

The little one stared at the food and licked her lips. Then she looked over her shoulder, quickly turning back. "Okay."

Piper moved the items on the seat to the floor then patted the leather. "Hop in. We'll go right up the driveway." She hurried around and drove them to the door on the back porch. Inside, Piper scooted a chair to the sink and had Emma pull up her sleeves. To her surprise, Piper saw dirt encrusted in the creases of her elbows.

"Emma, when was the last time you had a bath?"

"I don't know. I don't like taking baths anymore."

"Why not anymore?"

The little one shrugged. "It's cold."

Piper laid out the sandwich on the kitchen table and dug an apple out of the fridge. After filling a small cup with orange juice, she carried it to the table and sat beside her visitor. She watched the child stuff her mouth.

"Hey, slow down, honey," Piper forced open the small hand and pried out the chunks of meat from the sandwich. "You've got all the time you need, okay?" Emma nodded. They sat quietly for a moment. Piper itched to ask so many questions.

"Emma, sweetie, what did you mean when you said there's only the stream?"

"That's where Momma takes us when we have to clean up. It takes too long to make the water hot with the fire."

That answered absolutely nothing and gave her more confusion. "What's the stream?"

Emma tilted her head, brows down. "It's where the water flows. When it's warmer, we get fish there for supper there. Daddy is a good fisher in his bear."

Piper snapped back in her chair. Oh my god! "You mean you take baths in the river?" The small head nodded, taking a bite of apple. Piper got up and paced the kitchen. That wasn't right. What the hell was wrong with the mother? Did they not have water in their home? Did they not have any income? That would explain why the child was starving.

The girl slid down in her chair and burped. She covered her mouth and giggled.

"Did I just hear a burp from you, young lady?" Piper playfully stomped toward the table. "I'd think you were a boy. Only boys are so gross, you know."

"Boys are yucky," Emma said. "Especially when they're little brothers."

Piper gasped, putting her hands on her hips. "Yes, they are. They are horrible, aren't they." Emma giggled with her. Piper plopped into the chair she had sat in. "I have an idea. How about I make a *hot* bubble bath and you can play in the bubbles?"

"Really?" Large blue eyes shined at her. "Bubbles?"

Shit. Piper hoped the rental had bubble bath. If not, there was always the dish soap. Which might've worked better anyway.

Piper held her hand out. "Okay, let's go. I'll let you work the hot water."

In the bathroom, Piper peeled the disgusting clothes from the child. "You hop in the tub and I'll be right back, okay?" She poured a quarter of a bottle of lavender and vanilla aromatherapy bubbly bath wash under the faucet then gathered up the grubby clothes.

She would've preferred to throw them away, but she wasn't sure if the child had anything else to wear. Instead, she put them in the washing machine on deep wash.

Back in the bathroom, she sat on the floor next to the tub and scrubbed shampoo into baby fine hair. She wouldn't have been surprised if the girl's brown hair turned out to be blond.

"What were you doing out today?" Piper asked. "Playing?"

"I was looking for berries to eat. There's not many left anymore. All the animals have eaten most of them."

God, could her heart break into any more pieces?

"Is that what you were doing the first time we met?"

The girl shook her head but didn't answer. The

little one seemed to shrink into the bubbles. Something wasn't right.

"What were you doing?" Piper pressed for an answer. The girl shook her head, not meeting Piper's eyes. "Emma," she said a bit stronger, "why were you crying when I found you?"

The child sniffled. "I was going to run away."

Piper's hands paused mid-scrub then slowly started again. "Why did you want to run away?"

"I don't want to live there anymore. I want to go back to our house in town. I want to sleep in my bed and play with my dolly again."

Was her family evicted because they couldn't pay the mortgage? That had to be the reason. Shit. She had to do something to help these people. She had the money, but sometimes that wasn't enough. She needed to meet the parents. Hopefully this time, the father wouldn't try to eat her.

"How far is your current house from here?"

"We don't live in a house anymore," Emma said.

"Okay, is it an apartment or trailer?" Piper saw the child shake her head. "Where do you stay then?"

"We live in a cave."

The bottle of conditioner in Piper's hands

fumbled through her fingers and disappeared in the bubbles.

"I'll get it." Scrawny arms plowed through bubbles, pushing them over the tub's side. While the child searched, Piper sat in shock. People didn't live in caves. Even if they were half bear. The buzzer on the washing machine alerted her to the clothes being done.

"Can you finish washing up while I put your clothes in the dryer?"

Then girl nodded and Piper tried to smile at her as she climbed to her feet. Piper was sure the child could smell her emotions and didn't want to scare her. So leaving for a moment seemed the best option.

Anger built in her with each step down the stairs to the laundry machine behind the folding doors to the side of the kitchen. She threw the washer's lid up and fished the clothes from the bottom. Behind her, Zain came through the kitchen door. Piper spun toward him. His happy face fell instantly seeing her scowl.

He put his arms up. "Whatever I did, I apologize and swear never to do it again."

That would've been funny as hell if she wasn't so infuriated. She marched up to him and grabbed the front of his shirt and pulled him down.

She remained as poised as she could through clenched teeth. "They live in a fucking cave. If you don't fix this, I'm calling Child Protective Services and taking her and her brother home with me." Her fist holding his shirt shook. Damn, she was pissed.

Zain carefully loosened her fingers from his shirt then kissed the back of them. "Okay. Let's rewind a bit and tell me who she is."

"Emma," she spit out, "the girl in the woods whose father's bear nearly attacked me."

Zain frowned and nodded. "Is she all right?" I took a deep breath. "Why is she here?"

Piper held out the damp clothes. "Look at these." She pointed out the holes and threadbare patches.

"Where did you get those? Just throw them away. We have much better stuff than that."

"This is what she was wearing. And she was starving." Her anger was touching the boiling point as she threw the rags into the dryer and turned it on. "I swear to all that's good, Zain. If you—"

"Piper?" a sweet voice called from the stairs.

"I'm coming, honey." She turned on her heel

and walked out of the room, taking a deep breath to get herself under control. No bad emotions needed to scare anyone. The young one stood at the top of the stairs with a towel wrapped around her that went to her ankles.

"Did you get my clothes?" she asked.

"They're still wet, baby. You're going to wear one of my T-shirts until they're ready." Actually, the girl would stay in her T-shirt until she bought new clothes. Hopefully the town had a clothes store. Piper took the girl by the hand to her bedroom, then dug through her suitcase for the smallest shirt she had.

"Why is the alpha here? Am I in trouble?" The child shook and Piper didn't know if it was from fear or being cold after a hot bath.

"No, of course you're not in trouble. He's here to make sure everything is okay with me and you."

Emma nodded. "He used to come to our house all the time after my sister went away. But when we moved, he doesn't come anymore."

"Your sister went away? Where did she go?"

The girl's eyes turned to the floor and she shrugged. Piper slipped a T-shirt over the child's head and waited for stick arms to poke out each side. Geesh, the shirt almost reached the floor.

Coming from outside the room, she heard, "Are you ladies ready to go shopping?" Piper and Emma looked at each in response to the alpha's question.

"Shopping?" Piper said.

Emma's eyes got big and she grabbed Piper's hand. "Let's go. Shopping means we get new stuff and food." The girl pulled her to her feet. The strength in someone so tiny surprised her. Maybe the girl wasn't as fragile as she appeared. She was a shifter.

"Wait," Piper said, trying to pull back, "we can't go with you dressed like that. You need pants and shoes." They were at the top of the stairs.

"Nah, you're good," Zain replied. "We're not going far."

When Emma reached the bottom of the steps, she raised her arms toward Zain. "Hi, Alpha."

He scooped her up into a big hug, kissing her cheek. "How are you doing?" he asked, positioning her to sit on his forearm, arm around his neck.

"I'm okay." Her voice seemed sad, resigned.

He poked her belly. "You ready to get some new clothes?"

Her eyes lit up. "Yeah. I'm tired of wearing the same thing every day."

Piper followed Zain and Emma out of the door.

She was about to protest the no shoes but when he walked *past* the truck, she snapped her mouth closed. He kept moving downhill through the backyard then turned when they reached the open area under the main deck. She hadn't seen this part of the home, just the views from the top of the deck.

Underneath was a door that Zain opened and turned on a light. Piper heard Emma gasp and hurried to see what was in the room. When she stepped in, she felt like she'd entered a clothing department store in the mall.

Outfits of all sizes, mostly children's, hung on round racks and lay folded on tables. Shoes in all varieties lined shelves on the wall by size, again, most being youth. Blankets and sheets were stacked on tables along with some housewares.

"What is this place?" Piper asked.

Zain set Emma on the floor. "Look around a pick out things you like." He pulled Piper into his arms, snuggling her close. "This is the clan's secondhand store, I guess you can call it. Kids grow so fast and instead of throwing stuff away, it's donated here for others. Anybody can come in whenever they want and get things they need."

"I noticed the door wasn't locked. You trust

that nothing will be stolen?" Piper would never leave a door of any kind unlocked in the city. Not if she wanted to keep what was inside.

Zain chuckled. "Everything is free. There's nothing to steal. And I trust my people. If they need something, they can come here anytime they want."

Wow. She'd never thought about anything like this for this area. But she didn't know why not. People needed help no matter where they lived.

She looked around for stairs leading up into the home. "Does this have an entry to the house above?"

"No, when we built this alpha home for my mom and dad, I didn't want the security issue of someone trying to get into the home. If there was an entry, then I would have the door locked."

That made her feel a little better. Also made sense why they had to go outside to get in. When she saw Emma staring at what looked like senior prom dresses, she stepped away from the warm arms around her.

"I think I better contain the selection before she ends up dressed like a princess." Though the thought wasn't that bad. Every little girl deserved to have her dreams and play dress-up. But that was probably difficult when you lived in a fucking hole in the ground. Her anger flared to life, but she swallowed it.

Before she left, she'd have Emma and her family out of that cave and somewhere decent even if she had to adopt the whole damn family.

CHAPTER SIXTEEN

Zain leaned against a shelf in the secondhand shop below his mother's home. He needed to personally visit Ali and his "clan" in their new home. Zain had been very reluctant to grant Ali his own group land to live as they wanted. Not that he didn't want to give up part of the sleuth's property, but because he worried the new alpha had no idea what the hell he was doing.

Being a leader might look easy, but it wasn't. Especially when starting out with a brand-new group. There were so many things to do to make it happen, that it could be overwhelming. Zain had it relatively easy since his group had been established for a while and had money and investments to support everyone. What the almost dead town couldn't provide, the clan was able to cover.

They didn't have many costs. Just the normal utilities, food, and clothes, with insurance being the biggest cost for so many old homes and buildings. Luckily, they didn't need health insurance since shifters didn't get sick or hurt, for the most part.

He thought back to the last time he met with Ali. For a while, they met once a month to go over plans for building homes and necessities for the emerging sleuth. Ali always came to the alpha's home, never inviting Zain to his. At the time, Zain figured the smaller clan didn't want anybody seeing their poor conditions in the cave.

But Ali promised they would be out and in homes within a few months. It had been nine months. Eighteen months since the disappearance of their daughter, Linnea.

He sighed. That was such a dark time for the family and the clan. They had searched the mountainside and neighboring towns, but they found nothing. No trace of her.

That had been the only reason Zain agreed to

give Ali and those who followed him permission to have their own place. He hoped that giving them space would allow them to heal. But now he wasn't so sure that was working how he had imagined it would.

In the last several months, he and Ali had been too busy to find good times to meet, so Zain let it go thinking the small clan was moving along as planned. But now that he thought about it, there had been no construction of houses or anything else. No forest area had been cleared, as far as he knew. What were they waiting for?

On the other side of the room, he watched as his mate and the child searched through stacks and racks. Piper picked up a shirt and held it against the girl's tiny frame. She made sure the sleeves were long enough, that the shoulders weren't too wide. With pants, she checked the waist and length and verified the button and zipper worked.

The two worked well together. He'd bet Piper was great with children. He wondered why she didn't have any of her own. He knew she'd been wedded, but it wasn't a good arrangement. He hoped she wanted to have their own children. If she didn't, then he'd have to live with that. Of course, he needed to tell her she was his mate, and they were getting married and living in his house a bit higher on the ridge.

That could wait for a while. He had all month and needed that long to come up with a plan before dropping all that on her.

Emma gasped and he looked around to see why. The two females were toward the back where the bed and bath accessories were kept. A little finger pointed to a pink and purple blanket with a princess on it, sitting on a shelf. Piper pulled it down and the girl cuddled into it.

"With this," her high-pitched voice said, "when I sleep, the ground won't be so cold."

Zain now understood Piper's hot anger from earlier. His own lit, blazing enough to rile his bear at how the family must be living. Yup. He was going to a meeting very shortly.

Piper had found a large bag and had it stuffed with different things. The girls strolled up to him, hand in hand. The little one had on a good pair of jeans, sweatshirt, and sturdy hikers.

"Boy," he said, "I've never seen two women shop so long in my life. Did you get the whole store?"

Emma blushed and hid her face. "No, Alpha, we

only got this much." She pointed to the sack his mate held.

"Oh," he replied with surprise in his voice, "only that much." He glanced at his watch. "I think it's time we get you home before your parents worry."

Terror froze on the girl's face with tears quickly forming. She tore from Piper's hand, racing for the door. He snatched her up before she got out. She wriggled and fought his hold.

"I have to go, Alpha. Daddy will be so mad at me." Tears poured down her face. Intense fear came off her in waves.

He wrapped her up, calming her flailing arms and legs. "It's all right, Emma," he whispered, "you're with me. I'm taking you home, okay?" Her head nodded against his chest. Piper laid a hand on his arm, alarm on her face. He shook his head. They'd talk later. He took the bag from her. "Okay, let's go."

"Wait," his mate said, "you need your raincoat." Piper dashed out the door. He set the child on her feet.

Her wiped away a tear with his thumb. "You going to be okay?" She nodded. "Why would your dad still be mad?"

"Because I'm not supposed to leave the cave without him or Momma."

"You were out the other day. Is that why he was angry then?" Again, she nodded. The man couldn't expect a cub to stay in a dark, damp cave all day. Was he insane? Zain was beginning to wonder.

Piper came down with the bright yellow coat and slipped it on the girl. He kissed his mate for a long moment. Then pulled back, taking a snack container she handed to him. Her shiny eyes told him why. He whispered, "I'll return shortly," and kissed her cheek.

Her brows pulled down. "I can't go with you?" Zain shook his head just a bit, trying to let her know he didn't think that was a good idea. He worried that if she was angry at seeing the state of the girl's clothes, she'd flip out seeing the living conditions and not let the child out of the house.

"Oh, okay." Piper smiled the fakest smile he'd ever seen. "I'll be here when you get back." She squeezed his arm harder than he thought she could.

He returned the smile. "See you soon, love." He led Emma down the hill as she waved over her shoulder. That went better than he thought. Hopefully so would his next conversation.

On their way, they chatted about princesses and horses. He learned the mother was "home schooling" her and taking care of the toddler. When he spoke with Ali months ago, there were several couples.

"So the other males and females aren't there anymore?" he asked.

"No, Daddy and Mr. Schiller got into an argument and they left."

"How long ago was that?"

She shrugged. "A long time."

They came to a rope wrapped around trees about six feet off the ground. It marked the edge of the land he'd give to the new group. He frowned as he shook his head. The sleuth had never felt a need to mark boundaries. Land didn't belong to anyone; they were all renting.

Emma took him to the cave opening and when looking in, he froze. And was speechless. His anger roared to life seeing how the family—the children —were living.

"Momma, the alpha is here," the girl hollered with a slight echo deeper inside. The cave was large which gave them plenty of space. Large plastic containers held water probably retrieved from the river a short distance away. Blankets and pillows lay off to the side of the fire.

Winter would arrive soon, and he didn't see how they could survive with what little they had. He stepped inside and heard voices farther in.

"Emma, where did you get those clothes? They aren't yours."

"Yes, they are, Momma. The alpha and Piper took me shopping. And I got stuff for you and Chanie."

"But—"

Zain lifted the bag he carried. "It's fine, Marna," he said to the mother. The mother blushed and finger combed her hair out of her face. She looked a mess. Her clothes were raggedy, she was gaunt and the baby dirty, only in a material diaper.

He set the bag along with the food container next to the mother and squatted beside her. "Emma," he said, "come show your mother what you got." He met Marna's eyes, her tears ready to spill, but she held them back. He scooted the half sandwich and fruit closer to her.

Marna snatched it up and pulled the sandwich apart, feeding the baby pieces of meat and tomato. He wanted to grab them all and carry them out of this place. Give them enough food until they couldn't eat anymore. Put a solid roof over their heads with beds. He quelled his anger to not worry the young one beside him.

"Look what Piper helped me get." Emma pulled out the pink and purple comforter from the bag.

"That's beautiful, baby. Why don't you put it on your bed while I talk with the alpha."

Emma skipped to the other side of the fire where their "beds" lay.

The mother gave him a confused expression. "We don't have the money to repay you, Alpha. And you know Ali won't accept charity."

"These aren't charity. They are gifts from others who want to share. If it makes you feel better, I'll tell you I plucked them from the trash. Because that's where they might've gone."

"Ali will be mad."

As far as Zain was concerned, Ali could shove his anger up his ass. This was not a way to live.

"Marna, why are you here? Ali said he and your clan were going to build homes, have proper lives."

Her eyes stared to the floor, refusing to meet his gaze. "The others left. Went back to their homes. Ali can't do it all by himself."

"They probably returned home after seeing how wrong this is. Bears can live in nature, but humans will suffer. Why did you move from your home in town? Ali never told me. Was it because of Linnea's kidnapping?"

She nodded, the tears cutting clean streaks down her cheeks. "He's afraid something will happen to Emma and Chance."

"That's being paranoid, Marna. Linnea's death was a tragic event. We're all learning how to live in these modern times, and we're bound to make mistakes. Hiding in a cave away from society isn't the answer. We have to adapt and move on."

"Ali won't. He doesn't trust any of our neighbors and friends anymore. He hates the high school boys. I'm afraid when he sees them, he's going to shift to try to kill them. Being out here, away, is safer for everyone."

"Really?" he said, glancing at Emma and Baby Chance. "Everyone?"

"There's no internet, no phone—"

"Does your husband think that taking technology out of your lives will save your children? Emma could slip while in the woods, fall into the river and be carried away. You son could wander off and become lost. It doesn't matter where you live, our lives are at risk every moment of every day. A parent's job is to keep the children safe the best they can."

The mother nodded, wiping at the tears. "I can't leave my mate."

Zain sighed. Yes, he knew she wouldn't. He didn't want that as much as he wanted the whole family to move back into their home in town. He had made sure it remained in good condition in case they needed to return. That was a good call on his part. He would not allow them to be out here in winter. He stood.

"Tell Ali that I want to speak with him—"

A muffled roar came from the entrance of the cave and a large bear clambered in, a dead deer in its jaws. The bear dropped the animal and shifted. Marna scrambled to the carcass with a knife in hand. So that's how they'd been surviving—barely surviving.

"What do you want, Alpha?" Ali's voice shook with anger and his scent said shame.

"Dress and walk with me," Zain ordered, not wanting to get into a fight in front of the kids. After a moment, the two men strolled among the trees along the water.

Zain had a decision to make. Either be an asshole alpha and command them to move back into their home or take the mentor role and try to make the man see logic.

"What are you doing, Ali?"

"I am protecting my family and those in my clan."

Zain's brow lifted. "There are others still with you?" Ali looked away, not answering. The smell of shame growing. "Why do you think that is?" Ali remained silent, but Zain wanted response. "Why did the others move back into their homes?"

The smaller bear whipped around to face him. "Because they don't know what it feels like to lose a child. They don't know the frustration, anger, and pain of knowing you let down your family, your child. They don't understand the feeling of failure."

"How have you failed your family. You couldn't—"

"My daughter was taken from my home and killed by a stranger. I am the protector of my family."

Zain grabbed the man's shoulders. "Listen to me, Ali. You had no idea what Linnea was doing online. You had no idea who she was interacting with. She snuck out of the house in the middle of the night. Don't you think there was a reason for that?"

Ali stepped into Zain's face, nose to nose. "Don't you dare accuse her of anything. She was an innocent who that boy tricked into believing he cared for her."

"And you think by living in a fucking cave your family is safer? Look at them, Ali. They are starving. They are breathing air that is damp and moistened with moss. Animals live in caves, Ali. Are you saying you want to live like animals?"

With shifter speed, Ali threw a punch toward his face, but Zain caught it with his hand. His bear leaped forward under his skin. It wanted to tear this bastard to shreds for disrespecting the alpha. No one challenged the alpha in bear or human form. He took a deep breath and held back his other half.

Ali backed away, fear in his eyes, now realizing what he'd almost done. He turned and stomped toward the cave. "Sorry, Alpha, but I'm not letting my daughter be around boys, online or in town, who look at her as an object to play with. No, she will not go through what Linnea endured before she died."

The memory of the teen's tortured body

flashed in his mind. He couldn't blame a father for doing whatever necessary to protect the rest of his children. But he worried the children were more in danger in the wilderness than by any town member.

CHAPTER SEVENTEEN

Piper paced the kitchen waiting for Zain to return. An hour had passed, and darkness had engulfed the forest. But she knew he was safe. He was a freaking alpha bear. Nothing could touch him. Except her. She giggled at her silliness. God, she felt like a teen crushing hard on a movie star.

She'd put a pan of frozen stuffed ravioli in the oven for dinner and pulled out makings for a salad. As she chopped, she noted how quiet the place was. Sort of creepy with all the windows reflecting the inside of the home.

Bringing up her music app, she played her list which made her feel less freaked out. She belted out lyrics when she knew them and made them up when she didn't. Her hips rocked in time with the heavy beat. With a fork and spoon in hand, she pounded out the drum solo on the counter only getting half of it wrong.

When was the last time she'd done something like this—been happy enough to want to express it. For so many years, she cooked quietly while the cable news channel blurted out the good and bad in the world. Usually, new scenes came to her during this time. She could cook, brainstorm, and ignore her husband without a problem.

She looked up to see Zain leaning against the doorframe, watching her. She gave a short scream, the fork and spoon flying out of her hands.

"Jesus, Zain," she slapped a hand on her chest, "stop doing that or I'll have a heart attack."

He came inside with a big smile on his face. "I was just enjoying the show. I like the little shake thing you got going on." He scooted up to her, his hands settling on her hips and holding her in place as he rubbed his hard cock against her mound. God, the man was incredible and smelled so good.

"I smell pasta," he said.

"I put ravioli in to bake and thought about a salad to go along with it."

His grin turned wicked. "You can eat salad before dinner. I'll eat something else."

A shudder of desire shot through her. He breathed deeply and in his chest that purring vibration tingled against her. Hot hands squeezed her ass cheeks as a yummy tongue explored her mouth.

"How long until the ravioli is done?" he asked.

She leaned toward the oven and lowered the degrees. "About an hour."

He ran his hand down her back. "Make it two. I'll be right back."

She watched him head to the living room while she put a salad together and put it in the fridge. When she was done, she went into the living room and stopped in her tracks.

"What is this?"

There were a bunch of cushions piled up in front of the fireplace along with a movie at the beginning on pause. The room was lit by soft candles and the closer she got to the pillow fort, the more amazed she became. He piled bunches of pillows inside the fort, a basket of candy and a plate full of petite pieces of cake and sweets.

He grinned, walked over to her and grabbed her hand. "Come on. It's movie night in the fort."

She laughed but couldn't stop the flood of something way too close to love from filling her heart. Who was she kidding. She couldn't believe he was so thoughtful. So sweet and always thinking of her. Yeah, love was knocking at the doors of her heart and she wasn't sure she could stop herself from letting it in.

"I picked a good movie for us."

She crawled into the fort and he joined her. Leaning into him, she cuddled to his side. He curled an arm around her shoulders and held her close. The snacks and sweet were at their feet. To her shock, he opened some type of secret compartment on the side table next to the sofa and pulled out two tumblers with straws and two soda cans.

"What is that?"

"A hidden cooler."

"This place has it all," she gasped.

He chuckled, filled the tumblers, handed her one and then grabbed the remote to start the movie.

"The Conjuring?" She blinked at him with surprise. "I love this movie!"

He laughed hard and kissed her forehead. "I figured you would. I love how different you are."

She shouldn't feel so pleased with his words,

but she did. He said he loved that she was different. When had any man ever said that to her? Never. Just as the movie started to play, the sound of thunder and rain boomed from outside. Perfect.

They ate snacks and were midway through the movie when his hand slid over her thigh. She was instantly aroused. Her body wanted him. She'd been wanting to make a move since the moment Lorraine Warren had walked into the farmhouse and seen the haunted family.

She glanced away from the screen and turned her head to see him glancing down at her. The hunger and desire in his eyes warmed her from the inside.

"Kiss me, please."

He swooped down, his lips crashing over hers and pressing her into the pillows. The fire in the kiss heated her skin and had her whimpering instantly. His body lay flush over hers. She widened her legs and curled them around his hips. His crotch pressed into hers and she moaned at the feel of his hardness between her legs.

The kiss got more desperate then. Wilder. Harder. She raked her nails down his arms and to his T-shirt, yanking the material up to get it off him. He broke their kiss and met her gaze.

"I want you naked," she said, breathlessly. "Now."

A slow grin spread over his lips and he pulled back, sat on his heels and tore the shirt off. He tore it off. Her wildest fantasies were coming true. Then, as if to add gas to her flaming fire, he shoved his sweats off and moved on to her clothes. The outfit came off in the blink of an eye. She kissed him with almost as much desperation as he felt. His hands were all over her, his lips leaving a hot trail of kisses from her jaw to her breast and further. He licked and laved her pussy with his tongue, making her lose her mind for more. She was so turned on it took no time before she was gripping the pillows at her sides and wiggling her hips closer to his face, ready to come.

Legs shaking and struggling to breathe, she tensed, her pussy aching to be filled.

"Oh, god," she moaned. The orgasm took her quick, sending her over the edge and making her scream softly for Zain.

She opened her eyes to stars. He pulled her up and kissed her. She tasted herself on his lips and it did something to her. It was the rawest most primal kiss she'd ever shared with a man. The first man to give her an orgasm. She was already way too emotionally involved when it came to Zain, but she didn't care. So what? What did it matter? She'd leave with a broken heart, but she'd have amazing memories.

"Ride me, love."

CHAPTER EIGHTEEN

That's when Piper knew she never wanted to leave him. The way he called her love and caressed her cheek made her heart flip. She loved him. God. This was insane.

She nodded and kissed him while they switched places. Then she straddled him. She lifted, their kiss leaving them both gasping from harsh breaths. "I want you in me so bad. More than anything."

It wasn't a lie. He brought out emotions she'd never experienced before. Love. Desire. Passion. And possessiveness. She wanted Zain forever. For herself. Only her.

She caressed her nails down his chest, south to

his abs. "I don't know what all these emotions are. I've never felt so…much. Zain, I don't know what to do."

"Listen to your heart, Piper. Don't be afraid. I will never hurt you."

A slow smile spread over her lips. He was so sweet. So amazing. She wanted to keep him. Could she do that? Could she stay there and be with him? He had to ask her to.

He pulled her head down for a kiss. Even his kisses were amazing. So perfect. Her nipples grazed his chest and he sucked in a breath. It made her smile. It was empowering to get those reactions from him.

He grabbed his cock at the root, guiding it to her entrance. She held herself up by pressing on his chest. Her body was on fire. She needed him to douse her need. She lowered into a sitting position, impaling herself with his cock. They both groaned at the feeling. Pure bliss. She wiggled and pressed herself down even more, hoping to take in every single inch of him as deep as possible.

"Fuck!" He growled.

Her pussy clasped around his cock, squeezing him tight.

"Oh, wow," she murmured.

"Wow is right, love. You're fucking amazing. Being inside you gets more amazing every time."

She wiggled a little, rocking back and forth and sighing with the movement. "You're so deep. So deep."

"And you're so hot. Hot and sleek." He gripped handfuls of her ass and rocked her on his cock.

She dug her nails into his arms and shook her hips. At first, she rocked back and forth on him.

"Too slow," he grumbled.

She licked her lips and groaned with the feel of his cock rubbing her insides. Her pussy muscles clamped tightly around his cock.

He took control. She welcomed it and let him lead. Guiding her up and down, he helped her ride him faster, to come down harder, and to rock when she got all the way down so he could hit different areas inside her.

"*Yesss,*" she croaked. Her pussy fluttered. She was coming already? Zain was like a fucking sex god or something. As if reading her mind, he increased the speed. Moving faster when he lifted and dropped her. Her body tensed, her pussy clamping tighter on him.

He continued rocking her, guiding her up and

down his dick. Her head fell back, her eyes closed, and she breathed in short spurts.

She leaned down, kissing him and moaning by his lips. "I'm coming."

He nibbled on her jaw. "Come, baby. Let me see your beautiful body let go."

He rose and took her nipple into his mouth, suckling hard. A quick, harsh cry fell from her lips. She wiggled down to take him deeper. Her body shook with the force of her orgasm. Her pussy clenched around his length tightly as she rode her climax.

A loud groan sounded from his chest, shaking them both in the process. He continued to lift and drop her hard on his cock, until he suddenly stopped. His cock pulsed in her pussy, thick, hot and hard. Jets of cum filled her channel with his seed. It was fucking perfect.

"My goodness," she whispered, meeting his gaze.

"You're mine, Piper. Mine."

His words made her so happy. He wanted her long term. She wanted him too. He licked her chest up to her jaw and then kissed her hard and fast, while his cock continued to jerk inside her.

They fell back into the cushion, her body over

his, legs to either side of his hips, both slick with sweat and breathing ragged. She had so much to think about, but when he kissed her forehead and hugged her naked body to him, she closed her eyes and smiled. Later. Right at that moment she was going to enjoy being loved by Zain.

CHAPTER NINETEEN

In her robe, Piper served pasta and salad to her handsome guest at the breakfast table. Everything in her tingled. She felt so alive, all of her. Damn, how had she survived before this? This best-friends-with-benefits idea was exactly what she needed—to feel loved, to feel sexy, to feel wanted. Even though it was only pretend for a little while.

The plastic container that held the snacks Emma ate sat on the counter reminding her of the little girl. "When you took Emma home, was anything said? The parents were okay with her keeping the clothes and stuff, right?"

Zain cut through a pasta pouch filled with

spinach and cheese. He ate it, chewing without an answer. That couldn't be good.

"Why would the family move into a cave to begin with?" she asked. Maybe that answer was more important than the rest.

Zain put his fork on the table next to his empty plate. Elbows resting on the table, his hands clasped in front of his chin. He let out a sigh. Piper readied herself for a sad story.

"Emma had an older sister, Linnea," he started. She noted the use of "had" as in she didn't have a sister anymore. "She was a normal teen, liked in school, and got along with everyone. Apparently, though, she'd met someone online who had talked her into meeting him.

"Of course, her parents told her she couldn't leave to meet a stranger. So instead, she snuck out of the house after her parents went to bed. She'd never done anything to go against the rules, so her being gone the next morning was a big shock. We were able to follow her scent to the edge of town, then lost it. She must've gotten into a vehicle.

"Despite the possibility that she could've been a hundred miles away, the town went into search mode and hunted the forests in the area. After a couple days of nothing, one of the townsfolk who worked night security in another town told us about a red pickup truck he saw on the way home parked beside an abandoned building off the highway."

Zain picked up their plates from the table and carried them to the sink. She scooped up the silverware and glasses, following in his footsteps. She had questions but didn't want to interrupt. Unfortunately, Linnea's story wasn't unique in today's time. Too many young, unsuspecting kids had disappeared all over the country. She'd seen so many sad stories when she researched different topics. Each broke her heart a little more.

Zain took her hand and led her upstairs to the steps that went to the roof balcony. There, he sat and pulled her into his lap. This was one of the best things with Zain. He wanted her close even out of bed. She snuggled in to watch the clouds float past the bright moon. The river farther down the mountainside bubbled and rushed over its rocky bed.

She hated to ask, but..."I guess you found her in the abandoned building."

He nodded. "A human male, an eighteen-year-old, she met from another school had taken her there. We're not sure why, but we think he wanted to study her shifting."

Study? The word brought the image of a medical college class where a body with its torso cut open to learn about the inner workings of humans lay on a steel table. Her stomach revolted at the thought. Zain held her tighter.

"How did you catch him?" She didn't want to know any more about the corpse.

"His scent was easily picked up in the room, and his blood was on her claws. We brought in the county sheriff since we had a working relationship with him. He had his human forensics come in. They picked up fingerprints."

She asked, "Why would an eighteen-year-old have his prints on file with the police?"

"He'd signed up to go into the military. He was leaving the next day and thought he'd get away with it." Seeing her blank face, he continued. "Part of signing up is being fingerprinted. They had just been put into the system."

"Got it." She stored that little tid bit in a mental file for use later if needed. "What happened to him?"

"The sheriff took it to the Atlanta DA, and they

prosecuted. He was supposed to be in prison for the rest of his life."

"Was?" she asked.

"I heard the inmates killed him when they found out he'd tortured a 'child.'"

They sat in silence. She understood the father wanted to protect his family, but he was doing it the wrong way.

Zain kissed her forehead, scooped her up and carried her to bed for a long night of slow lovemaking.

CHAPTER TWENTY

Zain yawned as he stood in front of the chaos of teens at the pull-off on the highway. He had to admit it was *controlled* chaos as Spud directed everyone in getting the rafts off the truck, loading up equipment, and handing out safety gear.

With his mate leaning against him, he was the happiest bear in the world. She smelled of him from the sex they had in the shower this morning after all night of loving and talking about everything and nothing.

He didn't know how intelligent she was knowing so many different things. And he discovered that every time she said a cliché, she chastised herself mentally. He didn't think she even realized she did it. He'd take her, cliché-hating and all. He'd never read a romance book, but he was thinking about giving it a try. There was nothing wrong with a male wanting a little romance in his life. Especially when his mate wrote it.

When Spud handed the life vest and helmet to Piper, she held them out as if to say *Really, I have to wear this?* Spud turned on his heel.

"Not going there, Alpha. She's yours to convince. I'll learn from your mistakes."

Piper looked up at his with a raised brow. "What did he mean by that?"

He was about to ask which part but decided he didn't want to discuss any part right now. Nope, falling off a cliff would be safer. He had all month to get her to fall in love with him.

When the teens were ready and everybody geared up, including his mate, they headed for the creek not too far from the side of the road. Piper squeezed his hand harder than usual and he smelled the fear coming off her.

"You know," he said, "there's really nothing to rafting. Since you're in the center position, all you need to do is hold on and enjoy. The kids will do all the work."

"How many times have you been?" she asked.

"The older ones have gone several times. With the club and on their own. The younger ones, depends on how many years they've been with the group." He had complete faith in the teens' ability and skill on the water. Plus, he'd be tail on the first boat to do most of the guiding.

Ahead of them, the group reached the wide slow-flowing spot where the ground was almost flush with the water. Ideal for loading and taking off. Except this time, the flow wasn't so gentle. He'd thought most of the runoff from the rain would be gone by now. He'd thought the burned forest land would absorb more.

A couple years back, a huge forest fire took out a large chunk of the Smokies and Blue Ridge forests. Just about all the resort homes had burned to the ground. Pidgeon Forge and Gatlinburg evacuated in case the blaze topped the mountain and spread down. Not too long before this, the tragic events in Paradise, California, had consumed the news. The entire town had been decimated into ash. More than just the humans worried at that point.

The inferno had topped the ridge on the mountainside his clan's homes and town were on. But with the shifters assisting the firemen and women, they were able to create a firestop before any structures went up. The top part of the mountain was scarred with black sticks and colorless ash but sprouts of green had emerged in the past year."

Zain watched as the kids loaded the rafts without a single hesitation.

"Come on, Alpha. We're ready," Sally called from the first raft in the water. He helped Piper into the center of the boat. With four cubs around her and one up front with him in back, he allowed himself to remain calm and concentrate on his responsibilities as the tail.

He pushed off from shore and they were on their way. When the second group floated behind them, they all paddled downstream. The sky was cloudy but no thunderheads. If that were the case, he wouldn't have let them continue. The river down here was moving faster than he'd hoped in the first place.

His mate looked over her shoulder at him with a huge smile. "This is nice," she said. "It's beautiful here." Yes, it was. This was home to him and he didn't think he could live anywhere else.

They passed the overflow site where small boulders and large puddles lay. But today, those puddles had become an extension of the river. A dip in the rocky bed sent the raft splashing and chugging ahead.

Piper grabbed at the handhold on the seat to both sides of her. Her knuckles were pale, but she was secured where she sat. Their speed picked up with the river narrowing. The raft bumped off rocks and dipped, splashing refreshingly cold water into the boat. The kids squealed and screamed with delight.

Coming off a high point of water, the bow tilted up with water flowing over a boulder, tipping the raft before it slammed flat on the current.

"Alpha," Spud hollered, "the higher water has changed the line. It's not the same."

Zain heard the slight fear in the boy's voice. Shit. "Stay calm, Spud. Call it as you see it." The boy nodded repositioning for a more secure seating.

"Big water," Spud yelled. Instantly, they dove over an edge, the front going under sending a torrent of water over the front kids and spinning the raft. Zain heaved a sigh of relief seeing them all there when they surfaced. He needed to trust his team more.

"Dig in!" Zain thrust his paddle into the water,

searching for a way to hold his end of the raft so the current would push the front around. With the quick reaction of the paddlers, they corrected and were on their way.

During the turnaround, he saw the group behind them make evasive movements to avoid the same fate. Their faces were locked in concentration having realized this wasn't the course they had memorized in all their times through. Bumping off a rock, water splashed the crew and smiles and laughs broke out among them. They'd be fine.

"Boil," Spud hollered.

"Piper, hold on," he yelled, but she'd not let go of the straps from the first time he saw her grab them. The bow lifted into the air as if a plane lifting off the runway. For a second, they were airborne until they crashed onto the water with almost no splash.

His mate twisted around. She had the biggest smile and the excitement on her face was worth every splash of cold water. They careened through several breaking waves. If anyone was dry, they weren't now. After a few more bumps, they came to rest in another wide spot in the river. Everyone breathed easy.

"You did great, Spud," Sally said, slapping him on the shoulder.

The boy rolled his eyes. "I should be able to do this in my sleep. It's like a brand-new route." A smile spread on his face. "Pretty damn cool."

The second boat came up beside them. The kids chatted about what they'd just gone through while he held his hand out to his mate. She turned in her seat to face him.

"Wow," she said, "that's way more fun than the videos I watched. It's so wonderful here."

He laughed. Her eyes were shiny with happiness and her joy was abound. He'd done good. She looked so beautiful with her hair plastered to her head and her clothes drenched. She'd worn no makeup and she shined like an angel. He kissed her hand since that was the only part of her he could safely reach. Geeze, he had it bad for her. Always would.

"Alpha," Rubia called from the other raft, "we're ready to go."

He hated to let his mate go, but the sooner they were finished, the sooner they could be alone together.

"Positions," he called. Piper turned to face the front and the others settled in for the next stretch.

The other raft took lead, so they had it easier, just watching the group and copying their route or taking a better way if they got dumped.

Up front, Spud pressed his hand on the raft's surface, the rubber giving more than he would've thought.

Zain listened for the cues from the other raft until the water became too rough. He had to admit, he too should've been able to do this in his sleep for the dozens of times he'd been down it. But the pure adrenaline rush of not knowing what was ahead was a real boost, adding an element to his desire for his mate.

Last night, she was so soft, so pliant in everything he wanted to do. And damn, for someone who hadn't had sex much, she knew positions he'd never heard of, much less ever tried. Shit. He was starting to get hard. Not comfortable—

Screams ahead of their raft snapped his attention back to the world. The lead group had flipped their raft. Spud yelled directions to avoid the crash, sending them to the side.

"Shit," Spud hollered. "Hole!" The front of the boat dove under directly in front of a boulder, sling-shotting his team in all directions. Head popping out of the water, Zain searched for Piper and anyone struggling. The kids looked to be fine, riding the water feet first as they'd been taught.

The rafts were making their own way with everything that had spilled out. With all the helmets bobbing, he couldn't pick out which one was Piper. His bear was about to have kittens if he didn't have his hands on her in seconds.

"Piper," yelled out. The kids looked around at each other to see if she was among them. "Piper!"

"She's not here, Alpha."

CHAPTER TWENTY-ONE

Piper hadn't had so much fun in forever. She was drenched in cold-ass water but had enough adrenaline to power through a marathon. Well, a half marathon maybe.

Her fingers had been locked around the straps sown into the raft's material. Thank god for them. Without something to hold on to, she would've bounced around like a pinball.

As she settled in for the next stretch, the place she sat felt softer like air had been let out. She thought about saying something, but the other raft had taken off and the rapids were coming quickly. Watching the boat in front of them was scary and so cool. To see what would happen before she experienced it was thrilling. Until the lead raft turned up on its side dumping everyone out.

Fear exploded through her even though the teens were angling them away from the obstacle. Suddenly the front dropped and launched the back end up and over. Next thing she knew, she was submerged in freezing water and being pulled along. It was pitch black, but somehow, she could breathe when the water wasn't splashing in her face.

She didn't have time to think about where she was or what was happening. Her only thought was to not drown. The top of her head bumped against something when the water jostled her up. Her one arm was stretched out in front of her and her hand was wrapped around what felt like the straps she'd been holding.

Yes, that was it. She was under the raft with an air pocket where the floor had gone soft. The side of the boat tipped up, letting in light that showed her exactly where she was—still in the middle of the white water splashing off rocks and waves.

One good thing about her predicament was that the raft was keeping her from going underwater for long intervals. But that could change any second if her source of air went away. If she let go of the strap, she would immediately lose her air with no guarantee that the raft would float off her. She could get trapped underneath with no way of getting out.

This was the end. This was how she was going to die. In a water rafting accident. Not even she would write an ending like this. Though it was more exciting than most. She wished she could've seen Zain one more time. She was starting to like him. Like really *like* him. She felt more for him in her heart than she did her ex-husband.

Honestly, she knew she'd never loved Scott for sure now. He was such a nice guy with exciting dreams that she figured one day the love would be there. When he said he loved her, how could she pass up the opportunity to try? What if she never found another man who would love her. She didn't want to spend her whole life alone.

But that had ended up a disaster. All that time wasted where she could've been looking for someone. But if she hadn't married and suffered, then divorced, would she have ever come to the Blue Ridge Mountains, to the one rental that belonged to a man she could give her heart to? So many things she regretted—

The raft's front then side lifted off the water

and she slammed into what felt like a concrete wall. Her hand tore from the strap, leaving her draped over a boulder on the side of the river.

The water there was loud and violently crashed all around. She was high enough on the rock that only her feet remained in the water. She laid her head on the rock, closed her eyes, and thanked the powers that be for giving her a chance at a better ending to her life story.

Somewhere either behind her or on the far side of the river, she heard voices. She had no strength left to raise her head to look around or call out for help. The first boat had flipped also sending all the kids into the water. hopefully, they all got out. She probably would've been fine if she hadn't been trapped under the raft.

Hearing her name, her eyes opened to see the teens creating a human rope toward her. Several yards back on the other side of the water, Spud had an arm wrapped around a tree root exposed along the bankside. With his other hand, he clutched onto the forearm of one of the other guys. That boy's other hand latched onto one of the girls.

The chain worked its way diagonally across the water, flowing with the current, not across it. She didn't think even a grizzly bear could cut across water like this. It would knock anything over. Hell, the river had swept away boulders the size of cars. God, she prayed none of the kids slipped and went under. She would never forgive herself for being the reason someone else died.

A sudden weight flattened her against the rock then was gone. Beside her, Zain rolled onto his side. "Sorry 'bout that, babe. Didn't mean to squish you."

Her heart leaped with relief and joy. "Nice of you to drop by," she said.

"I was in the area. Thought it would be a good gesture seeing that you're a guest and all." He pulled her to him and kissed her hard. Damn, it was hot.

"Alpha," she heard. Sally leaned against a rock just behind them. The teens had created a shifter rescue rope. Unfortunately, she was too weak to even get off the rock. Not a problem when the alpha of a bear clan was nearby.

Zain grabbed her around the waist and hauled her against him. His hand stretched to Sally's. "Now," she yelled. The group muscled their way to the side, cutting across the current slowly, moving like a pendulum on its way down. Those not part of the chain stood along the bank ready to help anyone needing it.

Several minutes after leaving her safe rock, Piper lay on the dry ground staring up at the clouds. Many joined her, being exhausted from the rescue.

"How did you guys know to do that?" she asked one of boys, Brooks, nearby.

"We all talked about it once—what to do if someone got stranded or stuck somewhere. We've never had to use it before. Good to know it works."

She rolled her head to the other side where Zain sat holding her hand. "You raised some incredible kids."

He grinned, wiping her hair back. "They are pretty amazing, but I can't take all the credit. Our school is one of a kind."

She turned back to Brooks. "What are your plans after graduating?" she asked.

"Last summer I interned at an architecture business in Atlanta. They've offered me a part time position and paying half of my college. I hope to design buildings that are ecofriendly and weather resistant in non-conforming areas like the mountains."

"Damn," she said, "My graduating plans were to work at a fast-food joint and write at night."

Brooks laughed. "Fen is already studying to be a structural engineer."

"What does one of those do?" she asked.

"She'd help in the design of the building to make sure it was sound."

"Sound?" she asked.

Brooks explained. "Take a human body, for example. Fen would design the skeleton so it could take whatever was thrown at it. Me? I'd make it look like an eleven on a ten-point scale." The boy grinned. "We were hoping to go into business together sometime and build businesses and homes in the region."

If Piper didn't close her mouth soon, a six-legged critter might've wondered in. Impressed was not the word. Astounded worked better.

She asked, "Anybody else as ambitious as you two?"

"Spud's got a full scholarship to play football, but we all expected that."

Several feet away, Rubia raised a hand. Apparently, they all had been listening to the conversation. Damn shifter hearing. "I'm working with an interior designer after school who specializes in sustainable environments. She's awesome."

Piper didn't even know what that meant. She wondered if any of them knew Linnea. Had any of them been aware of what she had planned before her death?

The sky darkened and raindrops fell on the leaves above them. She was already drenched, so she wasn't worried about getting any more wet.

"What now, Alpha?" one of the teens asked.

Zain stood, helping her up too. "We're about half a mile directly south of town. Best bet would be to hike up there and have some parents drive us back to our cars."

Without a single complaint, the kids turned to the same direction and started walking. Well, someone had to stand up for herself. She raised her hand.

"I'm speaking for all the humans in the group." She got some chuckles out of that. "Some of us were not born able to walk a half mile up an almost vertical path after almost drowning. Any suggestions for those old folks?"

Valerian, one of the guys who seldom said much, spoke up. "You can ride."

"Oh," she said with sarcastic enthusiasm. "There's a ski lift or tram nearby?"

"No," he continued, "you can ride on Alpha's back. His bear is big enough to carry a couple of us."

Shock zapped her body along with un-ending embarrassment. Her face was on fire. Yeah, she'd ridden him a few times, but it wasn't in his bear form. Zain busted out laughing. Shit. He knew exactly what was going through her mind. She slapped him on the arm.

"Stop it before they figure it out," she whispered.

She heard a voice ahead of them say, "Too late."

Oh god. She was so not used to others being around. Writing was a solitary job.

When Zain wasn't at her side anymore, she turned to see him stripping his clothes off. She froze, hands over her eyes, but peeking through her fingers. No way was she missing out on this show.

"What are you doing?" she whisper-yelled.

"Going to let you ride…" he winked. "My bear this time."

Oh my god. Her face was melting from her

skull. This was not happening in front of a bunch of kids. She glanced back over her shoulder to see none of the teens were paying attention to the two adults. As far as she could tell. They probably heard—and understood—every damn word.

Piper watched as Zain shifted into his other half. It happened so fast. It looked painful and miraculous at the same time. Again, she had that issue with bugs flying in her mouth if she didn't close it.

"You want me to get on your back?"

The bear nodded, then with his nose, moved his shirt.

"I guess you would like your clothes when you shift back." A grunt was all she got back in response. Holy shit. What was she about to do? She gathered his clothes and stuffed them into the backpack he'd worn, then pulled her arms through. This couldn't be a good idea.

She stood beside him. "Zain," she whispered, "my leg doesn't go that high." He lowered to the height she needed. Damn, so much for that as an excuse. She hiked a leg over his back and plopped down as if mounting a horse. That wasn't too bad. She had ridden horseback a few times. All trail riding where she didn't have to drive, just hang on.

Zain stepped forward and she rocked backward, feet lifting. She grabbed a handful of fur and yanked herself down until she was almost lying on him. Then he was off. He zipped past the teens with a roar and they gave chase. She decided right then and there she would never try bull riding. Bear riding had to be the exact same. Every muscle in her body tried to hang on.

Much too long later, Zain finally slowed then stopped. She slid to the ground and lay there once again, rain falling on her. The kids passed by calling out they'd get rides to their cars and thanking the alpha for going.

"Remind me t-to never do that-t again," she said, arms spread out. With no sun out, her body had become frigid with the rush of air as Zain ran. Her teeth chattered

He laughed and took the backpack off her. "It's much better sliding downhill. Snow in the wintertime is a blast." He pulled clothes from the bag and started dressing.

She was sure it was fun but had no desire to find out. Shivering, she sat up. She saw Zain's frown. "We need to get you into dry clothes. I hadn't thought about how sensitive you'd be when wet."

"I-I'm f-fine," she stuttered. She hated being a problem to others.

Two of the kids—Spud and Rubia—had hung back. Both had the head positions on the rafts.

"Alpha, can we talk to you a minute?" the boy asked.

"Sure. What's on your mind?"

"The rafts," Rubia replied, "it felt like ours was getting soft after the first run but didn't think much of it until Spud said the same thing. Are they able to lose air? I thought you couldn't pop them."

"You're not, in theory," Zain replied. He slid his boots on while he pondered at the edge of a gravel lot. She could see structures telling her they were close to town, but she didn't know where.

"Either of you," Zain said to the teens, "sometime this weekend go down to the lake and fish out the rafts. We need to look at them to see what happened."

"Yes, Alpha." Both kids hurried away as she watched, wondering what that was all about.

"Oh," Rubia turned, "my mom said to tell you she loves your books and she'll be the first one to your event tomorrow at the bookstore." The girl waved and hurried to catch up with the football player.

She returned the wave with a genuine smile then wrapped her arms around herself. "You think s-something happened to the rafts while in the w-water?"

CHAPTER TWENTY-TWO

Standing in the parking lot next to Krista's store, Zain contemplated what the kids had just told him. He couldn't fathom someone sabotaging the rafts. That kind of stuff wasn't done here.

The thought that he almost lost his mate sent his bear into a tizzy. He closed his eyes and breathed deeply telling his other half that everything was fine. It was an accident and he would be more careful where she was concerned. Her being a human was completely different and he had to remember that and take care of her better. And right now, her teeth were chattering. Shit.

"Zain?" He heard a familiar voice. He turned to see Michelle from the bookstore in the gravel parking lot next to the building. She stepped away from the parked cars. "Piper? What are you guys doing? You look all wet. You guys come upstairs and let me get you some towels."

Zain gave his mate a hand to get onto shaky legs and they made their way to the set of stairs going up the side of the bookstore. He scooped his woman into his arms and felt her whole body shaking. Dammit, how could he let this happen. He had blankets in the rafts, but a lot of good that did them.

He carried Piper up the stairs and into Michelle's apartment home above the store. Michelle was waiting with a blanket and wrapped his mate and helped her inside. He went to the small kitchen and pulled out a coffee mug and opened the box of hot chocolate next to the coffee grounds. He popped the mug with water and powered coco into the microwave for a minute and turned to watch the girls talking on the sofa.

When the microwave dinged, he carefully took out the cup and carried it into the living room and handed it to Piper. "What are you ladies talking about?" Both females had smiles on their faces like they were going on about something they loved.

He sat and snuggled up to his mate. Michelle quickly got up and hurried away.

"I'll be back in a second," she said as she left down the narrow hall to the bed and bathroom.

Piper sipped the drink and moaned. "This is so good," she said. "Perfect temperature."

At least he got something right today. He'd have to rethink everything she did. He had to make sure nothing threatened her fragile body. Damn, he might have to tie her up inside his mother's home to keep her safe. Or for some other nefarious reason.

Piper glanced at him. "Whatever you're thinking, stop it. Save it for when we're home."

He was speechless. "How—I—You—"

Piper rolled her eyes. "You are so easy to read, Zain. I couldn't even write as obvious as you are."

Huh? That went way over his head. He was going to ask her to explain, but Michelle returned with several beach towels. She threw one at him.

"Here," she said with a scowl. "before you drench my sofa."

"Oh, sorry." He stood and tried to dry the cushion but it didn't do much, so he put the towel on the sofa and returned to his place with his arm around his mate next to him.

Piper said, "This is such a cool place. And you can't beat the commute."

Michelle laughed. "Yeah. After graduating college, I came back to town, not knowing what I wanted to do with myself. For about the past year, I've been hanging out here waiting to see if any opportunities became available. Krista rented this space to me and then asked me to work at the store."

"I love the rustic, minimalist look you have." His mate's eyes roamed the room.

Michelle laughed. "It's not on purpose. Believe me. If I had money to buy things, then I'd be in a big house with lots of stuff. Just gotta bide your time."

He wondered if his home was rustic, minimalistic. He didn't have a lot of shit in the big place. When he became alpha, the clan insisted he have his own alpha home since his mother was in the original. The community center was getting on in its years and had started to smell a bit musty, not to mention the ground had shifted and broken the foundation last year. He'd thought his place would become the default gathering location.

"Where you two hiking when the rain started?"

Michelle asked. She looked at his mate. "I thought you were here to write?" Something entered Michelle's mind and her cheeks blushed. "Oh, right. You two…" She stood again and went behind the kitchen bar separating the small spaces. She opened the fridge and bent over as if studying the contents.

"So, Piper," Michelle said, "You bringing Zain tomorrow?"

His brows raised. What was tomorrow? His mate looked at him and said, "I hadn't asked yet. I doubt he'd want to participate."

Still at the fridge, Michelle grunted. "Don't believe that for a second." She didn't say it loud enough for his human to hear. Piper stared at him as if waiting for an answer.

"Of course, I want to participate. What is it?" he asked. Michelle grunted again then closed the fridge door. What was her problem?

"See?" their hostess said, "he doesn't even have a clue, but he—" She abruptly stopped, eyes locking with his. "He's just too damn perfect, aren't you, Alpha?"

He floundered for words again. He wasn't used this kind of thing. And he sure as hell wasn't perfect. If he were, his mate wouldn't be a gorgeous iceberg at the moment. He remembered nobody had told him what was going on.

"So what is happening tomorrow?"

Piper laid a hand on his leg. "It's just a small book signing and talk I'm doing at the bookstore around ten in the morning for Krista."

"You're welcome to come, Alpha," Michelle said from the kitchen. "I'm sure you'd love to see her in action."

Thoughts of how he'd like to see her—naked and spread for him to eat—came into his mind. Oh, yes, he'd like to see her in action.

The shattering of a glass on tile jerked him back to reality.

"Dammit," Michelle mumbled. "Give me a minute to clean up and I'll drive you back home or to your cars."

When they stopped along the roadside location where his truck was, he thanked Michelle for the ride and helped his mate into his vehicle. He cranked the heat and fixed the vents on her to keep her warm enough. So he hoped.

With the windshield wipers swiping side to side, he headed back up the mountain. "I'm sorry you were put in danger," he said, trying to figure out if she was angry.

"It couldn't have been avoided, Zain." She took his hand into her and squeezed. "Besides, I've got a killer scene I can use."

He didn't smell anger or fear from her. Just the opposite—excitement and happiness with a bit of arousal mixed in it. And damn if that didn't make him instantly hard. Ugh! In wet jeans that was the worst. He'd have an imprint of the damn zipper on his cock for a week.

To make matters worse, she leaned toward him and laid her hand on his thigh. Fuck. He glanced at her and saw the look he'd come to know as the 'fuck me' expression from her. His foot pushed harder on the pedal. But the damn roads were too hazardous to go too fast, especially with rain.

"So," she said with a smile. Fucking A. She was teasing him and knew it. Damn, his mate was a little vixen who knew how to spark the fire in him. "I'm free tonight if you'd like to watch a movie or something."

Or something, please!

"Yeah, that'd be fun. I'm sure we can find something with a lot of action," he said.

She nodded. "I like action," she replied. "I like the scenes where it's one on one and they're rolling around and knocking shit down, they are so into it."

"Really," he replied, imagining them toppling kitchen chairs while they did it on the table. Her arousal dominated, filling the cab of the truck.

"Absolutely, and then one of them gets the advantage and just pounds away at the other. Harder and harder."

Shit. Harder and harder was right. Forget zipper imprints, it was now a tattoo. Finally reaching the rental cabin, he jumped out of the vehicle and carried her inside, not willing to wait for her to walk in.

Time for some afternoon delight.

CHAPTER TWENTY-THREE

She laughed as Zain lifted her from his truck and carried her inside. Yes, she purposefully teased him. God, it was so much fun. She'd never really done that before. Her ex would never play along, so she gave up early on.

When they got to the locked kitchen door, he cursed. Yes, she'd locked the door out of habit. She just laughed again. He was so adorable.

"Stop laughing at me, woman, before I take you right her on the lounger."

"Oh, let me get the keys," she said, snaking a hand under her as he continued to hold her in both arms. "In your pocket?" As she slid her hand into his pocket, which a bit difficult, but damn, if she wasn't playing this tease out as long as she could. He leaned his head against the door and groaned.

"Fuck, you're killing me."

She dug her hand as far as her fingers would allow. The keys were there, but that wasn't what she was after. She shimmied her wrist toward the inside of his thigh.

"Hmm, I can't seem to find those pesky keys. Where could they be?" Her pinky slightly brushed the side of his wide cock. His entire body shook, and his breath came fast.

"I'm going to break down the door in seconds."

Laughing, she pulled out the keys and found one with a label that said *Mom's*. She jammed it in the lock and twisted. The door flew open and Zain was inside, kicking the door closed. He carried her into the laundry room instead of the upstairs bedroom. What was he thinking? He had that sly look on his face.

He set her on the washing machine and pulled off her shoes and socks and tossed them into the dryer. He took a hand towel from a basket where cleaning rags were kept and rubbed it up and down her legs.

Goose bumps rolled along her thighs. Then it was her clothes. They were both naked in the laundry room and she wanted nothing more than to be fucked then and there.

"Come, love. Let's get you in a warm bath," he said, leading her to her bedroom.

They were in front of her bed when she pulled him to a stop and lifted up on her toes and pulled his head down. "Kiss me, Zain. Make me yours. Bath later."

"Are you sure?"

She grinned and nodded. "I want you deep inside me. I want to be yours. Only yours."

CHAPTER TWENTY-FOUR

Zain knew he had to control himself. Fucking her like an animal wasn't the best way to make her his mate, but fuck if he didn't want to do just that.

"Lay on the bed and let me see you," he told her.

She crawled on the bed, wiggling her ass as she moved up on the bed. Then she flipped onto her back. She spread her thighs wide, showing him her slick sex. The scent of her arousal filled his nostrils and pulled a low growl from him.

"Is this what you want to see?" There was a flirtatiousness in her voice he hadn't heard before and he loved it.

He yanked his bear back and crawled up the

bed to her. He stopped when he reached her sex and inhaled.

"I'll never tire of your delicious scent."

"Really?" She asked, looking down at him, her head on a pillow.

"Never." Then he swiped his tongue over her folds. "Mmm," he groaned. He glanced up from her pussy. Her eyes were half-closed, her lips open and huffing out a breath. "Once you come on my tongue, I'll fuck you."

She gripped his hair, her nails dragging through his scalp and letting him know how lost she was in his touch. God, he fucking loved knowing she was his.

All his. He pressed the tip of his nose on her clit as he drove his tongue in and out of her. Every lick brought on new moans from her, and his own grunts wouldn't stay quiet.

"Holy fuck!" Her muscles locked, legs tightening around his head. Her climax approached and he couldn't wait to taste her release.

He slid two fingers over her entrance, wetting them with her honey, and then drove them into her channel. He didn't stop. He fucked her quickly, his moves driven as if he were grinding his hips into her sex. She gasped and groaned.

"Don't stop," she begged. "Don't ever stop."

He fingered her and flicked his tongue on her clit in quick circles. Fast. Faster. Until he knew she was about to fall from the edge, and he would be the only one there to catch her.

"Oh god!" Her climax came with a loud scream from her, her body shaking and her pussy grabbing at his fingers, sucking them tight. She held his hair in a grip and her hips convulsed as she tried to ride his fingers through her orgasm.

Her hips rocked back and forth on his face, her hot honey dripping down his hands.

He gave her a moment to catch her breath. Then he got on his knees on the bed and moved his body closer to her.

"I need inside you," he growled.

She scooted down, lifting her hips up to him in offering.

He clearly saw her pink folds and slick sex calling for his dick. It was time to take what was his. His mate.

"That's it," he said, his gaze on her tight, sleek pussy. "Now, let me in."

He pressed the head of his cock into her, his gaze moving up to her face and watching her suck in a breath. Her gaze slowly crawled down his body to watch him slide into her.

He took a pillow and shoved it under her ass. She gasped and gripped the bedding when he held onto her hips. One slow, smooth drive and he was in her. Filling her. Getting even harder as he felt her pussy tighten around him like a hot, wet tongue.

"*Yessss*," she muttered.

He pulled back to slam back in. Harder. "You're tight and hot and I can't get enough." Another pull back and she gasped a soft moan. "I'll never be able to get enough," he grunted with a hard drive, "you're mine."

He bit his fingers into her thighs, lifting them and holding them flat against his chest. "More, love?"

She groaned with each deeper drive. "Yes." She rocked her hips. "Always more."

He pulled back and thrust deeper. He took every inch of her with little control. His bear needed her, and Zain wanted her more than his next breath.

He watched her puff out air and her breasts jiggle as he pounded hard into her. It was a beautiful sight. He could spend the rest of his life with his cock inside her and never want to leave her body.

She whimpered, "Oh, god. I'm so close."

He nodded. "I know love. I'll take you there."

He drove harder and faster into her. He pressed a thumb on her clit, flicking it back and forth at the same time he fucked her. She whimpered, her pussy contracting around his cock. He knew her orgasm was coming fast.

"Fuck!" he growled, his cock hot and deep inside her. His climax shook him to the core. As he came, shooting jets of hot cum into her, an electric shudder raced down his spine.

He let the bear out for a second and used his claws to lightly scratch at her hips, leaving his mark and mating his woman. Piper was his. Forever.

She screamed his name, her pussy sucking on his cock and contracting so hard, she drank his cum deep into her channel. He'd be lying if he didn't admit that was the best sex of his life. Being with his mate was better than anything else in his life.

CHAPTER TWENTY-FIVE

At a quarter to ten the next morning, Zain lifted four folding chairs from the back of his truck and tried to shake the rain off them before taking them into the bookstore. The waterworks hadn't given up. He thought how ironic it was that not long ago, they were so dry that fire engulfed the trees in seconds. Now, they had so much rain you couldn't set a branch on fire.

On his way down the mountain into town, he noted a couple places where the ground had let loose and slid down several feet. Those were mostly in places where the trees were thin, not much to keep the erosion down. He just hoped that higher up on the ridge where the fire had ravaged the area that enough foliage had regrown to strengthen the earth.

He carried the chairs inside the back door to the parking lot, then was directed up the stairs to the second floor. Climbing to the next floor, he saw his little mate helping set up the space where she was to give her presentation and book signing.

Looked like Jessie from the bakery brought over finger cakes, cookies, and tea. Seeing the amount, Zain raised a brow. There was enough for sixty people. He expected more like ten from such small towns. But what the hell did he know about romance book presentations? He planned to stick around for a while just to watch her.

Seeing Piper by herself, he scooted closer to her. "How are you doing," he asked.

She snickered. "Just as well as when you left my bed this morning."

He hmmed in her ear—better than saying what went through his head which was *let's fuck more right here*. "We'd still be there if not for this community gathering on your behalf. It's good for everyone to get to know you, though."

She leaned back and looked at him. "Why do you say that?"

His eyes got big. Oh shit. He hadn't really

meant to say that. Damn, keeping his mate a secret was near impossible. Some of the kids might have figured it out yesterday, but they wouldn't say much. He had to cover his own tracks here.

"Oh, you know," he said. "We don't get famous people around here much. It's exciting for us mountain folk."

She snorted. "Whatever. I don't consider myself famous. Yeah, I've sold a few million books, but I'm still the same girl who was cheated on by her husband of many years."

He couldn't help the growl deep in his chest. Her ex-husband was a stupid piece of shit to let her out of his sight. But it was fortuitous for him.

The main door downstairs squeaked open and women began filing in and up the stairs. Many knew each other, many from his clan. They gathered around the snack table and talked and laughed. The occasional glance swept over his mate and him.

"You going to stay?" she asked him.

"Sure, why not. We need to take the chairs back to the center when this is over." Besides, how boring could it be listening to his mate talk about a book while he stared and fantasized about what he was going to do with her when they got back to the cabin.

Krista stood at the front of the room and hollered for everyone to take a seat. With a quick count, he came up with forty-nine people. Seemed like a good turnout. Krista welcomed everyone and introduced Piper to the group. She came up front and he stood in the back, leaning against a low bookcase.

"Hi, everyone," Piper started. "I'm really excited to be here. I don't think I've ever gotten as warm a welcome from anyone as from here. And on such short notice. I can't thank you all enough." When everyone was quiet, staring at her with expectant faces, she asked. "Anybody have any questions?"

Half the arms in the room raised. The smile on her face lit up his insides. She was so beautiful. She pointed to the first lady in the first row. The woman squealed and bounced up to face her and the crowd. Eh, excited much? he thought.

"I've heard the saying that authors write what they know," the visitor said. That made a lot of sense. How could you write about something you had no clue about?

Then the woman leaned forward as if to whisper to the entire upper floor. "So...Well, you

write the hottest sex scenes so does that mean..."
Most in the group twisted in their chairs to look at
Zain.

Not only did he freeze in place, but his bear
lifted its head with a *huh*. Every woman up there
had turned to look at him now. Were they staring
at him because they think he had sex with her?
How did they all know? He popped off the bookcase and stood straight, his face burning like he
was bent over a campfire.

"I, uh," he stammered, "I should go downstairs."
He scooted toward the railing and missed the first
step, almost falling. "Excuse me, ladies. I need to
check something."

He hurried down and out the back door then
leaned against the wall to let his face cool. Damn,
he should've known better than to be around a
bunch of women. That was the easiest way for a
male to get into trouble.

Toward the back of the parking lot, he saw a
female in a raincoat with the hood up walking to
the building. Must be a latecomer. Not caring to
be seen, he inched over to the side of a pickup
and left the female undisturbed. When she
reached the door, he realized it was Michelle.
When she pulled the door open, she had some-

thing in her hand. He couldn't tell what. It looked like a cake server.

He glanced at his watch and wondered what to do with himself now that he'd changed his plans. He hopped into his truck and dried off a bit with a towel from the back seat with his extra clothes. Best thing to do for his mate was to go grocery shopping. He wanted to get more salad stuff and he needed eggs to make another of the chocolate cakes she enjoyed.

He drove a block down and parked outside the small food market. The first person he saw inside was Ali's wife and two children. She pushed a cart with the infant strapped into the front section, the girl holding to the side of the wire basket. When Emma saw him, her face lit up and she ran to him. The mother scowled and looked away.

"Hi, Alpha," the girl said, "Dad brought us to the grocery store. Isn't it great?"

His heart fell. Dirt coated her arms and face. He wanted so badly to make their situation right, but it wasn't his family. He couldn't force them to do what he thought best. But them purchasing vegetables and other nutritious food would ease his worry a bit.

"What are you going to get?" he asked, squatted down to her eye level.

She shrugged a shoulder. "I don't know. We can't get much. Dad said we don't have any money."

That was another thing with Ali. After his older daughter died, he quit his job before moving out of his home. Zain had offered him some financial assistance, but, of course, the proud bear wouldn't accept the offer. Fuck, what a mess this whole situation was. He knew Piper hated it just as much as he did—not being able to make things better for them. He didn't know how to get through to the father.

"Where is your dad?" Zain asked the child.

She shrugged again. "Don't know. He dropped us off and went somewhere."

He wondered where that was. Was he getting supplies that would benefit them? He sure as hell hoped so.

"I know," he said, "what one thing in this store would you get if you could get anything?"

The girl clasped her hands. "I'd get the candy bars Piper has. She gave me one the first time."

"Can you find one for me? Do you know where the candy is?" he asked. She nodded and was off.

Zain stood, shaking his head. He dug around in his front pocket for change and pulled out almost two dollars. When Emma came back, she held a protein bar with blueberry filling.

"Oh," he said. "You like those?" She bounced on her toes with the bar clutched to her chest.

"They're my favorite now." With her smile, he saw she had a missing tooth. Probably no tooth fairy for her.

"Pull open your pocket," he said then poured the change into the coat opening. "Use that to buy your bar. If your mom or dad say something, tell them that you helped to clean Piper's home the other day and that's your money you earned for it, okay?"

Her grin was so real, so deserving, his bear came to the surface wanting to claim her as his own and take her to his den to protect and provide for her. But his human side knew that wasn't possible.

Her smile fell and she glanced back at her mother who still had her back to them. Then with shiny eyes, Emma laid a small hand on his arm. "Alpha, can I come live with Piper?" she whispered. "I promise to be really good and will help clean the house for real."

He tilted his head toward the floor so she wouldn't see the anger and sadness flash across his face. Trying to hold his emotions in check, he placed his big hand over her tiny one on his arm.

"I'll tell you what," he said after fighting his bear for the child's custody, "how about you and I visit later, and we'll play some games? How does that sound?"

Her lips smiled, but her eyes didn't. The child knew what that meant. She'd probably had nothing but disappointment in her life since the loss of her sister. He told her she better get back to her mother before she worried. He watched her run off. She wore the hikers and jeans she and Piper had picked out.

He hurried through the store to gather the few things he needed, including a whole box of the blueberry protein bars, and set it all on the conveyor belt in the check-out lane. He also grabbed a hundred-dollar gift card. After paying for everything, he asked the cashier, one of the teens, to pack the bar box with Marna's other items when she checked out.

With no one in line behind him, he stepped out in search of the girl again. When he found her, he waved her over, the mother again frowning.

"I gave you the wrong amount before," he handed her the card. "This is what you earned. Tell your mother to use it all, okay?" He ruffled her hair then headed out of the store before Marna could argue with him.

Outside, as Zain put his bags in the small space behind the seat, Ali pulled in and parked. Time for an alpha discussion before shit hit the fan. More than likely, his own shit. He took a deep breath to keep it cool and nonconfrontational.

"Hey, there, Ali. Good to see you getting more than just wildlife for your family." After the words left his mouth, Zain winced a bit. So much for nonconfrontational. Ali got out of his car and stood as tall as he could. Still several inches below the alpha.

Anger rolled off the man. "Look, Alpha Lock-wood, I want what is the best for my family and keeping them away from those males is the best."

"What males?" Zain asked.

A scowl marred the man's face. "The teen males that are always out on the street."

Zain had no idea what the man was talking about. There were no males, or females for that matter, always on the street. "Do you mean those who pick up trash in the town every other day after school? Those who work in town after classes to bring in extra money for their family?"

Ali's face blossomed red, his fists opening and closing. "Just keep that female away from my child. I've smelled the human on my daughter several times. I don't care how famous she is or how many come to see her talk."

Now the man was close to crossing the line. If he meant Piper as the "human female," then things just went downhill. The man even knew where his mate was at the moment. Was that what he'd been doing? Spying on his mate?

Zain's eyes narrowed. "You mean the one who feeds your starving little girl? The one who gave her a bath and clothes because she'd had neither? The one who seems to care more about the child than her father?"

Ali stepped forward putting his chest within a hairsbreadth from his own. Zain had to admit the bear had balls. "Yes. The girl is mine." His voice was more growl than words. "I will kill anyone who tries to take her from me."

At the threat, fur rose through Zain's forearms, paws forming where his hands fisted at his sides. Nobody threatened his mate. Nobody. The grocery glass doors opened and Marna and Emma walked out with a packed basket, Emma munching on a protein bar. When seeing them, the mother stopped and grabbed the girl's arm.

Zain sucked his bear in not wanting to scare the children or cause a scene. When he could talk again, he said, "Emma did some work for me in the forest and she was paid for her time and labor." He completely lied, but he didn't want the father destroying the food because he viewed it as charity from someone. "The money she *earned* bought the groceries."

Before anything else pissed him off, Zain walked back to his truck. He left the parking lot but kept an eye on Ali to watch what he did. If he hit his wife, the female and children were going in his truck right then. Surprisingly, Ali helped load the sacks into the trunk, then hugged his wife for a long moment. Maybe things might be all right.

As he pulled out, he saw Rubia park her truck out front of the community center. In the bed, Zain saw what he thought was a river raft, but it was mostly deflated. What the fuck? He turned their way and parked behind them.

"Hey, Alpha," Spud said, getting out of the passenger's side of Rubia's vehicle. "Come see what we found." The teen pulled one of the boats onto the sidewalk. He tossed it around looking for something. "Here." He fingered a rip in the sturdy material that shouldn't be there according to the manufacturer.

Rubia dragged the other raft from the truck's back. "We found another just like it in almost the same place on this one too."

Could it be coincidence?

Rubia shrugged. "It could be a fluke that both have holes. We did travel down the same path, but river rocks just aren't sharp enough to tear this material."

"And the water was deeper than normal," Spud comments, "There could've been a stick or something strong enough that both of us didn't see."

Not likely. Not where the holes were. These were placed where they wouldn't be seen. Both kids were experienced leads and had shifter-sharp eyes. So that really left only one option.

Had someone sabotaged the rafts?

Why?

CHAPTER TWENTY-SIX

The presentation being an awesome success and mentally draining, Piper laid back on the sofa with hot cocoa in hand. Zain would be there as soon as they returned all the chairs to the community center.

The women she'd met were the friendliest group she'd ever spoken to. They wanted to know more about her personal life than her book writing. She couldn't lie to them with a made-up story about a nonexistent lover. That just felt wrong. She told them she was recently divorced after years of marriage.

Then began an AA meeting but for divorced women. They talked about how their male mates could drive them up the fucking wall, but true mates loved until the end. No cheating, no second guessing, no wandering eye. And hot in bed for a very long time.

She listened as they discussed mates. Damn, she couldn't have made a more romantic notion about a husband if she wanted to. But of course, they weren't completely perfect. They were men, after all.

She lost count of the times the women praised Zain, the clan *alpha*, the top of the pile, if she didn't know. Anybody who mated with him would be the luckiest woman ever. He was so sweet and charming and blah, blah, blah. The women talked him up to be a Greek god, making sure she understood how well he was raised.

If she had questions about him as a perfect partner, they were totally blown out of the water. Cliché, dammit. She wondered why some female shifter hadn't snatched him up already. Piper was sure whoever this woman was would have to be drop-dead gorgeous, long legs, and big boobs. Perfect damn teeth you see only on toothpaste commercials. And hopefully, she'd have a brain and big heart.

Except for the last two, Piper had no chance of being the perfect woman for the alpha. But she never figured she'd be good enough for him in the first place. She was completely astounded he'd agreed to the friends with benefits. She'd ride the wave as long as she could then go back to her solitary writing life.

The door to the kitchen opened and the man of the hour strolled in. He was so smooth and controlled as he moved. Like a tiger when stalking through the jungle. So sure of himself without consciously trying. At the same time, his heart was big enough to care about not only friends, but the children who weren't even blood relations.

For such a big man, he was gentle with his hands and soul. Hell, he could cook and bake. She could live off his chocolate cake and lemon bars alone.

When he reached her on the sofa, he leaned down and kissed her hot enough to curl her hair, and her toes. His hands cupped her face, touching her more. She felt him kneel on the floor in front of her, never breaking their connection. This wasn't just a normal kiss.

This was an *I need you* kiss. *I don't want you to leave* kiss. An *I want to share my life with you* kiss. She'd never felt anything like it. Her heart burst, taking in what he was giving and returning all she could.

He laid his forehead against hers. She licked her lips and smiled. "So, what's up?" she asked.

He chuckled, still on his knees before her. "I met Spud and Rubia today. They'd fished the rafts from the lake at the end of the river."

"Oh," she said, "I wondered what would happen to them."

"Each had a rip in the rear area hard to see under a flap. Technically, I wouldn't think it would be possible to naturally have a tear there."

"Wait," that caught her off guard. "What do you mean? Not naturally?"

He sighed and sat back on his heels, taking her hands into his. "After examining the rafts...Piper, you need to understand something about me. I am an alpha which makes me overbearing, overconfident, and protective as hell."

Yeah, the woman at the signing had mentioned all those traits. But Zain made them sound bad as opposed to the ladies. His seriousness worried her. Was he telling her their friends relationship was over? It wouldn't surprise her. He deserved the best and she was wasting his time.

He growled. "Dammit. I'm not doing this very well."

She didn't want to drag this out. She had writing to get to. Laying a hand on his cheek, she said, "Zain, it's okay. I get it. I knew it wouldn't last. But, honestly, I had hoped it would last longer, but..." she shrugged, trying to hold tears back.

His head shook. "What are you saying? No, whatever you're thinking, it's not that." She took a deep breath to swallow the lump in her throat. "Piper, I'm trying to say that I could've really lost you yesterday. I don't think the rafts were accidents. I don't know the purpose, but in the end, you'd be the one hurt the most being human."

"You're talking about the rafts? I thought you were wanting to stop being *friends*."

Another growl escaped him. He cleared his throat. "Sorry about that. My bear didn't like the idea you presented there. Actually, we—my bear and me—want you to be more than friends."

Her heart kicked up a notch. "More?" The cabin was silent except for the rain dropping on the windows and roof. "Like what? Best friends?"

He cleared his throat. "Piper, this may be too soon for you, but a shifter knows when they've met their mate. There's no questioning, no second guessing. They are certain they've met the one for them."

She'd heard all that today and more. Why was he telling *her* all this? He could leave her anytime he wanted.

"Oh," she said, "you met your mate." Now she understood.

He sighed. "Yes. After all these years, finally."

She sat staring at him, trying not to be ugly to him.

"You don't get it," he said. "Piper, you are my mate."

She startled, throwing herself back into the cushions. She wanted to tell him that he was wrong, incredibly wrong. His mate was gorgeous with thick hair and perfect teeth. But he and the women said a shifter knows when they've met their mate. Could it really be? Was that the reason she couldn't love her ex? The man she was meant to be with knelt in front of her.

Her eyes narrowed. "Are you sure? This isn't a joke on the human thing?"

He laughed. "No, my love. This is a shifter thing. You are my mate and I want you to be with me for…forever. I can't stand the thought of you being away from me even between this house and mine."

She grinned. "Is that why you've been here just about every night?"

His smile turned wicked. "That and more is why I'm here. I will protect you with every fiber of my being. Being mine, someone will think twice about trying to hurt you. I will kill anyone who tries."

She wasn't sure if that was the most romantic thing she'd ever heard or the most psychotic. "Okay," she said. "Let's give it a try. Can't be worse than what I've lived through. At least this time I know I will be in love with my man."

"And he loves you now." He leaned forward and kissed her. Damn, maybe she was already in love too. Seeing that it was early afternoon, she figured now would be a good time to get started on the whole mating thing. Some of the things the women said about their shifters, she could never put in her books unless she changed genres to erotica.

Zain lifted her then a loud thud on the front deck turned their heads. Someone banged on the door so hard, she heard it splinter.

"What the fuck?" her mate growled. "Piper, find someplace out of sight for a moment."

She wanted to know who was threatening to break down her door, but then she could wait for that info too. She hurried to the other side of the stairs and peeked over a step toward the living room.

Zain threw the door open, ready to pounce. When he jerked to a stop, she wondered who it was.

"I want my daughter back right now. You have no right to keep her," a growly voice said..

Oh, him. Emma's father. Zain told him she wasn't here.

"She has to be here. We've been searching for her for hours," Ali said.

"She was at the grocery store not too long ago," Zain replied.

"And she disappeared after that. Someone has her."

"Now, Ali don't jump to conclusions. She's probably just in the forest somewhere and doesn't realize how long she'd been gone."

"In the rain?" he questioned Zain. Piper made her way to Zain. She remembered the first time she met Emma. It had rained and she was drenched in her yellow coat. During the bath, the girl had confided that she was going to run away. Oh my god. Had she done it?

"Zain, we have to look for her. How far can a child walk…" She turned to Ali. "How long since you last saw her?"

"Four hours."

"And you've looked for her around here?" she asked. "Can't you smell her."

Zain put an arm around her. "Not in rain like this. All scents are pretty much destroyed by the water."

"Did you check the waterfall?" she asked. Piper stared out the front window, down to where the river flowed. In the daylight, she noticed for the first time how high the water was. It rimmed the top of its banks. Oh god, what if she fell into the river? Her knees weakened. "Zain, we need to find her now."

CHAPTER TWENTY-SEVEN

In the community center, Zain had laid out the maps on the tables several of the others had set up. The fact that the last time he had these maps out was to search for a daughter of the same family wasn't lost on him. He prayed that the end result would be much different.

Before they left his mother's home, he put their emergency plans into motion by calling his beta who then called the others on his list, who in turn called their own list of people. This was something the community had created after the kidnapping of Ali's oldest child. They hadn't had to use it yet. No better time to test it than in the middle of a crisis.

Almost the entire town had shown up when he

reached the center. Many were part of the last search and were ready to go. He sent them off in different directions. His explorers team arrived, and after getting permission from their parents, they went out to search the west side closest to the waterfall. Many had shifted before going out.

Hours had passed with no news from anyone. Volunteers floated around the main room in the center handing out towels to those returning and taking calls. But with phone coverage being spotty in the mountains, not everybody could call in to report. You could get a signal in a location, but move a foot to the side and it was gone.

The bakery had brought over some food and drinks for the volunteers and those checking in and going out. The remnants of granola cookies sat on the table in front of his mate. He'd insisted Piper stay in the center to help in the coordination. She didn't know the area and would be better off by his side, though he didn't tell her that part. Knowing his caring mate, she would've insisted on helping. This was best for all.

Zain also had Ali bring Marna and the baby to the center. He wanted the whole family there and waiting for when Emma was found.

The continuous rain worried him. He didn't

like the looks of the river. It had never overflowed in his years here and earlier today it had reached the bottom of the bridges.

On the way down the mountain, he saw several more slides where mud had flowed over a drop off of rock. Nothing big, but such a flow could easily bury a person if caught in front of it.

The main worry right now was the waning light. They only had about an hour with all the storm clouds.

His mate picked at the cookie crumbs as Ali paced in front of the door. "You know," she said, "I once read about a family who had moved to a rural area to get away from the crime in the city. Not long after they moved, there was an active shooter situation where the wife was killed."

Zain looked at her. "No happy ending there?"

"Nope," she replied. "I just find how ironic it was that they left what they thought was a crime area for a *safer* place." She glanced at Marna holding the baby. The woman lowered her eyes. She understood. It was Ali who Piper aimed her story at, and of course, he said nothing in response.

His mate continued. "Zain, now that we've

determined that we are mates, we should talk about having children."

His eyes bugged out. Was she serious? He took a seat next to her. "I didn't want to rush you, love. But, yeah, I'd love to have as many as you want."

"I don't have children, so I've done a lot of reading on how to raise a balanced, happy child."

That's good. He didn't have much experience in dealing with diaper bound cubs. "There are—"

"I'm sure," she cut in, giving him a look he didn't understand, "but research shows that nurture is stronger than nature when it comes to children."

"Uh, yeah," he said. "What does that mean?"

"Well, Zain, I'm glad you asked." Why was his mate talking louder than normal and what was up with the fake voice? "That means we as parents have a duty to be involved in our children's lives. The more we know about them and their surroundings, the more we can protect them. Don't you agree, Zain?"

"Uh, yeah." He wondered if she was feeling ill.

"I also read this article that said if you give your child ten minutes a day to just talk to you, then they may become more open and willing to share their feelings and what's happening around them.

Do you think ten is enough? Maybe fifteen minutes each day?"

"Uh, yeah." What the hell was he supposed to say. He had no clue what she was going on about.

"And," she continued in this strange act, "I came across this magazine with a story on how we, the adults, need to manage our own feelings. If we are mad because you did something dumb, then you might take that out on your family. Plus, by handling you own confrontation, you're teaching your child how to correctly deal with their emotions. Did you know that?"

He narrowed his eyes. Was she really expecting him to answer? "Well—"

"Of course," she drawled on which meant she didn't want him talking for some reason, "the most important thing to being a parent is to tell your children every day that you love them." These last words were spoken in her real voice. "If they don't feel loved because we as parents don't interact with them because we're busy, then they will seek that love elsewhere."

Ali spun around from his place at the glass door. "I do love them. They are my children. How can a parent not?"

Zain wasn't sure what was happening here.

His mate turned to the man. "Do you tell her that or do you assume a five-year-old knows how a parent feels?" Ali stood with his mouth open. "How many five-year-olds do you know who understand what anger is? How do they know it's not because of them? Their first inclination is to think they've done something wrong. Any idea how guilt can cripple emotional growth?"

"I do not take my anger out on my family!" he hollered, stomping toward the table. Zain tensed to dive over the barrier if needed. Nobody was to come close to his mate.

Piper nodded. "I can tell as you all but attack me for something I didn't say." Ali stood fuming. "Look, Ali, all I'm saying is learn how to give your love to those you care for. Let them see how they make you feel. Not how the world makes you feel. If all you hang onto is hatred and anger, then that's all you can give. Kids, and spouses, sense these things and think they are to blame. You don't want that. Show them love."

Ali glanced at his wife and toddler huddled on a blanket in the corner. Zain scented the sadness, fear, and longing from that side of the room.

Ali locked eyes with Marna. He said, "That's all

I've been able to feel since...I don't know how to make the pain inside me go away."

"Talk to your mate," Zain said. "Tell her everything you're feeling. Let her help you carry the load. That's what mates do." Then it dawned on him what his smart little mate had been up to. Never would she cease to amaze him. He watched as Ali sat with his mate and took her hand in his. Hopefully, they would work this out while the others searched for their child.

Michelle came in the community center's front entrance with a platter. He wanted to thank her for her help, but instead of bringing the tray to the table, she'd glanced at him then handed it to someone else to set down. She stayed across the room near the family.

His mate slumped in her chair and rubbed her head. He scented pain coming from her.

"You okay, babe?"

"I have a headache coming on and my migraine meds are in my suitcase."

"Do you want me to go get them?" he asked. His mom had suffered the same ailment for a while, and he knew how debilitating they were.

"No," Piper said, "you're needed here to assign

new locations when search crews return. I'll be okay for a while."

Michelle approached their table. "Piper, if you want, I'd gladly drive you up to the alphas' home. My car is at the store." She smiled. "I haven't had you all to myself yet. I have so many questions I want to ask."

Piper stood. "Thank you, Michelle. That would be great. And I'll tell you all the secrets you want to know." She turned to Zain and kissed him. "I'll be back shortly."

He watched as the two women walked away. Something niggled at the back of his brain, telling him not all was well. Another rain-soaked couple walked in and cups of hot coffee were rushed to them. Both came his way to report in. By their expressions, he knew more than a lost child weighed on their minds.

"Alpha," Raisa said. Her mate shook his head as a silent sign they found nothing as he sipped the hot liquid.

"How's it look out there?" Zain asked.

Sam scowled. "I'm worried about the streams higher up the mountainside. We haven't had nonstop rain like this in years. Not sure how stable the ground is in the burned section."

Zain agreed. He knew the dangers of the slopes right now. But he didn't want to pull the searchers until he absolutely had to. They only had an hour's worth of light. Even though his bears could see in the dark, he wasn't sure if risking the overflowing creeks and river was wise.

Vanessa, Michelle's older sister, threw the door open and rushed inside. She glanced around as if looking for someone. When she met his eye, she visibly relaxed, but still seemed worried as she came over.

"Alpha, can I talk to you a minute. Privately?"

That surprised him. "Sure. Let's go to one of the back offices." He opened the door leading to the hall and followed her through. After the door closed, Vanessa entered an office and paced. "What's wrong?" Did she have information on the missing girl?

"It's my sister, Michelle," she said. "Something isn't right."

"What do you mean?"

"The past few days, she's seemed...agitated. She's growly and like she was back in school. I just went to her apartment and it was trashed. Furniture thrown around, cabinets open with everything on the floor."

That didn't make sense. "She was just here with cookies from the bakery. She seemed fine. How was she in school?"

Vanessa chewed on her lower lip. "We didn't tell anyone because she appeared over the guy. She met one of the frat presidents and became obsessed with him. She stalked him and caused some issues with his girlfriend that put the girl in the hospital."

"Okay," he replied, not sure what he was to do with that information. "Is she stalking someone in the clan?"

Vanessa scrunched her brows down. "Yes, you."

"Me?" Zain stepped back, shocked with her news.

"Don't worry, Alpha, she only told me about you two hooking up all the time."

"Excuse me?" he blurted. "She'd made it clear that she wanted to...spend time with me, but I told her no. I was waiting for my mate."

Vanessa stared at him, disbelief on her face. "She said you were going to ask her to move into your home. That you wanted to mate with her but were waiting for some reason she never told me."

He was speechless. Where had this come from? Michelle was always touchy feely, but he thought that was just how she was when she returned from school. It seemed that she had found ways to be around him. Like delivering the bakery goods to the center. But she was just being the nice person she seemed to be.

Then it clicked. Vanessa was telling him this because the college boy's girlfriend had been hurt by Michelle. Which meant his own mate could be in the same situation.

"Michelle is driving my mate up to the rental," he said.

"Are they alone?" Fear resonated in Vanessa's voice.

"Yes." Zain rushed into the main room of the center, headed for the door. "Sam," he hollered to the man still sipping coffee, "I need to leave. Can you cover this?" Sam was instrumental in the previous search and Zain trusted him to give new locations to those who returned. Which reminded him that the teens hadn't returned yet. Shit.

"Sure, Alpha, go," Sam replied. "I got this."

"Wait, Alpha." Zain stopped to see Ali hurry toward him. "I'd like to go with you. I owe an apology to your mate."

Zain wanted to tell the man it could wait, but that would take time as they discussed why it wasn't that important right then. So Zain waved him on. He could sit in the back of the crew cab.

On their dash to the truck, he called Piper's phone, but got her voicemail. Either she didn't have a signal or couldn't answer. His bear pushed him to move faster.

The rain came down even harder than earlier if that was possible. Since the river bypassed the town, he wasn't worried about massive flooding, but many streams coming off the mountain drained directly into the underground water system for the town. Could that overflow? He didn't know.

Spinning out on the pavement, he raced for the turnoff to the twisty road taking them uphill. How much of a head start did Michelle and his mate have? Not long. The wipers swept water from the truck's windshield, but not enough for him to see clearly. It was that time of day when headlights did little to help or hinder their progress. But he knew these roads by heart.

Two turns away from the driveway, the truck began to shake. "What the hell is going on?" Zain rounded the bend and was met with a wall of mud that slammed into the vehicle, taking them downhill. The bed of the truck slammed into trees and the mud flow parted around them. Within the longest moment of his life, the ground stopped moving. They were buried up to the door handles

"Everyone all right?" Zain asked. Both passengers mumbled they were fine. In the woods to the side, flashlight beams bobbed and bounced, coming their direction. When he recognized Sally, he breathed a sigh of relief. The teens were safe at least.

"Alpha, oh my god," the girl shouted, gaping at the scene. The others stopped at the edge of the piled mud a few yards away.

Vanessa hiked a leg and put her boot through the windshield. From there, they climbed out.

"We need to get to the old alpha cabin," Zain yelled through the rain. "Piper could be in danger."

CHAPTER TWENTY-EIGHT

Piper sat quietly in Michelle's car as her new friend navigated the dark road up to the cabin rental. She expected to be drilled with questions about her characters and plot lines. Unlike her sister, Michelle had no issues with how the stories played out.

But Michelle hadn't said one thing yet. The woman seemed preoccupied.

"Everything, okay?" Piper asked.

The driver smiled. "Perfect. Just noticing how high the water was under the bridge. Anything caught up in it would be swept out to the Tennessee River, never to be seen again."

Piper's brow raised as a chill raced down her back. That was a strange way of saying something.

But Michelle had a point. The water had been high. She wondered if the section of waterway below the house was flooding yet. When they reached the driveway, she breathed out a relieved sigh. They had made it.

"You want to come in," Piper asked. "I'll only take a minute, but I'd hate for you to wait in this weather."

"That would be great," Michelle replied. "I haven't been in the *old* alpha home since I'd been back."

Piper noted the stress on the word "old." As opposed to the "new" alpha home she wondered. Did she mean Zain's house?

They ran from the car to the back deck then inside the kitchen. When she flipped the light switch, no lights came on. "Oh crap. The power is out again. Zain came over and started the generator the last time the lights went down. I have no idea how to turn it on."

"That's fine," Michelle said, "I'll just hang out here."

"I'll be just a minute." Piper felt her way through the unfamiliar rooms. She could see more as her eyes adjusted, but just enough to not stub her toe. When she climbed the stairs, the little light she had vanished with the bedroom doors closed.

Behind her downstairs, she heard a noise from the direction of the living room. So much for Michelle staying in the kitchen. Her friend had said she hadn't been in the home for a while, so she was probably looking around with her shifter vision. Lucky dog, well, bear.

Piper scooted along the wall, passing the stairs up to the rooftop access, to the first door which was to the room she stayed in. The other three bedrooms she'd hadn't even looked at. The inside of her room was a bit more illuminated, but not much. Bending down, she felt for the edge of the mattress and worked her way around to the other side where her bags were.

She found her big purse and dug around. Ugh, she remembered why she seldom carried the damn thing with her. It was filled with all kinds of shit. You never knew when you'd might need a bandage, lip gloss, hand sanitizer, or key fob with a small light.

She pulled out the set of keys and squeezed the gadget that lit up a few feet around her. Cool. Her meds were at the bottom of the black hole of a purse. She popped one into her mouth, then rounded the bed, fob light held in front of her. In the hall, she noticed that one of the doors to a bedroom was cracked open.

Had that always been that way? She remembered the creaking sounds she heard when she was downstairs that night reading her horror novel. That was ridiculous. No one was in the home even though she didn't lock the doors earlier since Zain didn't. She swallowed hard.

Deciding she didn't want to know if anyone was in the room, which there probably wasn't, she hurried down the steps. Coming off the stairs, Piper had the small light pointed outward. When she rounded the corner, a sting hurt her hand and the fob hit the floor and slid into the darkness.

"What the hell?" she said.

"Sorry," Michelle said, standing much closer than she expected. "Well, not really."

Piper backpedaled, slamming her heel against something, and crashed to the floor. "Jesus, Michelle. You scared the crap out of me." There came no reply to her comment. She looked around for her friend, not seeing her nearby. "Michelle?"

"Over here," the woman called from the windows overlooking the front deck. Her voice sounded different to Piper. Dull. Lifeless.

"You okay?" Piper asked. "I'd offer coffee, but we need power for that."

"Let's go for a walk down to the river," Michelle said, turning to her.

"What?" She couldn't have heard right. It was pouring rain and friggin' cold at that. Her friend's hand wrapped around her wrist and pulled her toward the door.

"I said let's go outside. I don't want to mess up the floor."

Instinctively, Piper yanked her arm free. Something wasn't right. "Mess up the floor how?" As she stepped back, she reached behind her, fingers touching her laptop sitting on the table beside the sofa.

"Come on," Michelle said, reaching out for her, "I don't have all night. Besides, I have plans to fuck your memory from my mate's mind."

Piper's jaw dropped. "I don't know your mate. I thought you lived alone."

"That is temporary. Zain was going to ask me to move into his home, but you're in the way, taking his attention from me."

"Whoa," Piper said, sliding her hand under her computer, "Zain said I was his mate."

Michelle advanced on her. "He's mistaken.

You've been fucking him and now he thinks he belongs to you. But he doesn't. He's mine. I've been trying to make him realize that since getting back in town. He's a hard-headed alpha." Piper saw her friend's arm extend toward her and she slung around her laptop, smashing her attacker in the head.

Michelle recoiled, surprised. Piper ran, slamming her shin on the coffee table, landing on the floor again. In a flash, the crazy woman was on top of her, hand around her throat, claws poking at her flesh.

"Dammit," Michelle said, "I told you I didn't want to get the floor bloody." No. Piper discretely remembered "bloody" had not been mentioned earlier. "Now, let's get to the river so I can toss you in." Now, Michelle's comment in the car about the river washing away everything made sense.

Piper fought to stay on the floor. Michelle growled. "Stop resisting. This will be easy." Did the woman think Piper was stupid? Of course, she'll fight. Around them, the floor began to vibrate. Earthquake was the first thing to come to mind. But she didn't think they had those here. Then what was it?

"Fine," Michelle snarled, raising her claws. "I'll get the floor messy then."

From the darkness, a small bear charged the crazed bitch, knocking her from Piper's body. With one swipe of small claws, her enemy's throat was ripped out. She'd been caught by surprise and died before she knew what was happening. Hearing the same sounds as she did when Zain shifted, she waited to see who had come to her rescue. To her shock, a naked Emma stood where the cub had been.

"There you are. People are looking for you."

Emma lowered her head. "I don't want to live in the cave anymore. I want to live with you." A tear rolled down her cheek.

The vibration she felt a moment ago became stronger.

The windows in the kitchen and living room exploded in. Piper couldn't see what smashed the windows, but the image of an avalanche came to mind. They had to get to higher ground. "Upstairs," she yelled, grabbing Emma's arm and running.

Climbing the steps, her body was thrown to the side. Her shoulder hit the wall, but she kept going. They had to get to safety on the roof. That was as high as they could get. Her footing made her stumble many times; she wondered what was happening to cause that.

Up the second set of stairs and onto the roof, Piper realized why she couldn't stand up—the mud had pushed the house from its foundation and was slowly dragging the structure to the river.

She gripped onto the chimney and pulled Emma to herself so both of them could cling to whatever they could. Rain beat down on them instantly soaking her through. Her hands quickly became numb from her death grip on the stone chimney.

Under her, she felt the house crumble, windows crushing in and wood snapping. One thing she had never researched was how to survive a mudslide by surfing it on a roof. This was a first and a miracle. With a screech, they came to a halt and the loud rumbling changed from the movement of dirt and rock to the rushing of water.

The mudslide had taken them down to the river, stopping just before being swept away. Terror washed through her at the realization she and Emma had survived the frying pan, but were going to fall into the fire any second.

On the chimney, flashes of light illuminated the

stone then were gone. When she turned her head, she saw what could've been flashlights bobbing in the woods on the other side of the water.

"It's the alpha," Emma said, pointing toward the lights, "and Daddy." The girl jumped up in her hold, shouting and waving her arms for her father. With the roof being slanted and wet, Emma lost her footing and went down.

Piper had never moved as fast in her life as she did that second. She threw herself into a head-first dive and snatched the girl's flailing arm before she plunged into the river. Somehow, the child was able to climb up and over Piper's body to a spot on the shingles where she sat.

Piper scrambled backward with Emma's help to where they both were safe. She heard voices over the sound of the rushing water but couldn't make out the words. Emma called out that they both were okay and that somebody needed to get over here right now. Piper smiled at the girl's confidence and bravery.

But Piper didn't have the heart to tell the little one that nobody, shifter bears included, would be able to cross the raging torrent separating them from their rescuers.

At that second, a loud pop echoed and the

remaining house beneath them shifted closer to the water. Piper lay back to stay flat on the surface, Emma wrapped in her arms.

If the guys didn't figure out a way to get to them quickly, there wouldn't be anything left for them to rescue.

CHAPTER TWENTY-NINE

Zain, Vanessa, Ali, and the six teens stood motionless, rain pounding them, as they watched the cabin slide down the hill, crumbling from the bottom up. Zain had never seen anything like it. After the house came to a stop, an upside-down car zipped through the water past them. It tossed in the current, slamming into a boulder and tumbling along.

"That's Michelle's car, "Vanessa shouted. Zain put a hand on her arm in case she tried to go after the vehicle. If anyone was inside, it was too late to try to get to them. He didn't need another member of his clan getting into danger and needing a rescue. His mate and Michelle were hopefully somehow safe in the mangled mess of wood and mud on the other side of the river. Though he didn't see how.

Over the weather, he heard a high-pitched voice ring out. "Daddy," came from the home. How was that possible? He ran uphill closer the bank-side and squinted through the rain. There on the roof, Emma slid down the side, screaming, with Piper right behind her. His mate grabbed the girl's arm just as her legs dangled over the edge. They climbed back onto the roof and he nearly passed out from cardiac arrest.

His mate was the only one to start his heart, and apparently, she could stop it just as easily.

"Alpha," Sally called out, "we need your help." He followed the teens up the river away from the house.

"Stop," Ali yelled. "We have to save my daughter."

"We are," Spud hollered, wiping water from his face.

Ali grabbed the football player's forearm, fur erupting below his elbow. "Don't you touch her. I'll kill you."

Spud shook him off. "What the fuck is wrong with you, man? Do you want your kid alive or do you want to bury her too? I was close friends with

Linnea. It tore me apart to know she was gone. You weren't the only one to grieve her loss. And I'll be damned if I'm going to let another die if I can save them." Spud puffed up his chest. "So stay the fuck away from us until your daughter and the alpha's mate are safe."

Zain stopped next to a gawking Ali, putting a hand on his shoulder. "Trust them, Ali. You'd be surprised how the younger ones think if you got to know them."

The teens stood in a group assessing the situation when Zain reached them.

"No," Val said, "Sally I know you're strong, but this is beyond what the rafting current was. Spud is the only one strong enough to carry both females and hold on to get back."

Immediately, Zain knew what the group had planned. They had pulled it off once when saving his mate. Could they do it again with conditions much worse? If they failed, they would all be swept downstream, possibly not surviving. Not even shifters could breathe under water.

"Let me bring them back," Zain offered. He was the alpha and the one responsible for everyone's safety.

"Alpha," Brooks said, "we need you and Linnea's

dad to anchor. It will take us all to reach the other side.

A scream came from his mate and the house moved beneath them, bringing them closer to the water. Soon the current would be able to catch timbers and drag the remaining structure under.

"Let's go." Zain hollered to Ali. "We need your help. Follow me." Zain took off his leather belt and wrapped it around his wrist, buckling the rest around an evergreen tree. After testing the hold, he put his arm out to grab onto Val. Ali did the same, securing himself to Brook's arm.

From there, both boys grasped onto Sally who had taken her belt and tied herself to Rubia. Zain wondered why the teens had decided to go with two anchors instead of one. Fen grasped Rubia's arm after she'd lashed herself to Spud. Then they entered the water.

Their feet were swept up and Zain saw the reason for the double anchors. It took both Val and Brooks to keep the girls from being yanked in.

Spud and Fen fought their way diagonally across the water to reach the other side. Zain watched at the young alpha took his T-shirt off and put it on the child to cover her nakedness.

Piper tied up the bottom since the shirt reached the ground. Emma could walk now if needed.

Zain glanced at Ali next to him holding onto one of the teens. The father's fear-filled eyes were fixed on the action taking place across the river. He couldn't tell if rain or tears rolled down the man's cheeks. Maybe both.

Spud signaled and the girls pivoted to pull the line back to this bankside. Zain felt the strength in the bond between the kids; not only physically, but mentally, spiritually. They willed the human chain to reach this side with sheer determination. When bodies touched solid ground, there was a collective sigh as the ties and belts were undone.

Ali scooped his daughter into his arms when she raced to him. She held onto her father like she never wanted to let go. He hoped they would remain that way for the rest of their time.

The ground began trembling and the sound of snapping trees came from higher on the slope.

"Ali," Zain yelled, "take us to the cave."

"This way," Ali said, and they all ran to outpace the tons of earth and trees rolling down from the destroyed sections of the peak. Settling safely inside, a fire was made from the stacked wood and blankets wrapped around those who were cold.

Zain held Piper in his lap, refusing to let her up for any reason. He was going to hold her until he and his bear were convinced she was safe.

As they sat around the fire, Ali stood and circled to Spud and the boys.

"I want to apologize for my actions earlier," the father said. "I didn't trust you even though I should have known better."

Spud got to his feet, several inches taller than the father. "That's understandable with the situation Linnea was in. But you have to know we are each our own person. Just because one is a piece of shit doesn't mean we all are." Zain rolled his eyes at the boy's choice of words. He would never get through speech class without offending at least one person.

The football player put his hand out. Ali accepted the gesture of forgiveness. When the boy returned to his spot on the ground, the young set of eyes met his. Zain gave him slight nod of approval.

Yeah, the sleuth's town might be dying, their population dwindling, but those who were raised here were going to do good in the world. He couldn't be prouder than that. And with his mate by his side, he would protect and guide the clan till it was time for his children to take over.

And by the slight change in his mate's smell, the first of their children would be here sooner than later.

EPILOGUE

P iper stood on the outskirts of town with the rest of the residents. Well, what was left of the town, anyway. All she could see for the most part was a field of mud and half buried trees. No homes, no winery, no grocery, no community center. The bookstore and bakery remained only because the terrain of the mountain's side directly above them banked up, keeping the flow from spreading that far.

The weather had finally let up, the sun coming out for the first time in days. The crowd looking on the devastation remained quiet, almost mournful. Zain had told her that Sam had evacuated the whole town before the slide reached the town. She was grateful the old bear realized what was happening before it was too late.

But now nothing remained. The area was a blank slate of devastation of the land. Brooks stepped up beside Zain. "You know, Alpha, there's this great spot up the highway that would be perfect for a winery."

"Yeah," Fen said, "with some modern building materials and proper layout, there's enough room for a residential subdivision and other buildings there. It's a great location."

"Well," Zain replied after a moment, "guess you guys need to get drawing if we're going to have our new town up and running before next tourist season." The kids walked away with huge smiles on their faces, already making plans.

"Sorry about your mom's homes," Piper said.

"Eh, she didn't want to be there anyway. To many memories. Now, like the rest of us, she'll get a new home made for her."

"Alpha," Ali called out, cutting through the crowd with his family in tow. "Speaking of homes, I'd like to buy one for us."

Emma gasped in her father's arms. "Really, Daddy? We can live in a home again?"

He smiled at Piper. "I think so. I've done some

research and found someone who is going to help us all move on. She's helped lots of families who've lost loved ones." Emma hugged her father then wiggled out of his arms and ran to her. Piper groaned as she lifted the youngster onto her hip for a hug.

"You're getting married to the alpha, right?" the child asked. Piper's eyes popped wide and she fumbled for words.

"Uh," she glanced at Zain who shrugged like he didn't have a clue what the child was talking about. Ha. She knew better. He probably put the little one up to it. "Yes," she said, "if I haven't killed him by that time."

"Good," Emma replied. "I want to be the first to babysit your babies. I'll feed them blue candy bars like you did me."

Her knees almost gave out. Talk about jumping the gun by a mile.

Ali took his daughter and they melted into the crowd. Piper stared a hole in her mate's head. What was that all about? Was that his way of seeing if she'd marry him?

"Meh," Vanessa said, coming up beside her. "Don't worry about that. I've got your back."

Got her back for what? She wanted to know

what was going on, but mostly, she thought Vanessa hated her.

"And just because you don't write your stories correctly doesn't mean we can't be friends. I'm still your biggest fan."

Piper swallowed the sudden swell of emotions. "I'm sorry about your sister," she whispered.

Vanessa lowered her head. "Thank you. I'll miss her, but she was getting really weird before you even showed up. I should've paid more attention to her issues when she was in college. But I thought she'd be okay." She was quiet for a moment before continuing.

"Michelle said something that you might understand better than I did." Piper stayed silent waiting for when Vanessa was ready to talk about her deceased sister. "She said something along the lines that she hoped you couldn't swim. Any idea what that means?"

Zain squeezed her hand. His glance at her said he knew exactly what was meant by the cryptic statement. Piper turned back to Vanessa.

"Nope. Have no idea what that means."

Her new friend nodded. "I just wondered. Okay, just let me know when you want help. I can do whatever you need. Hopefully, the new alpha home will be ready before then." Vanessa hugged her. "Congrats." Then she walked away.

Having enough of this strange talk shit, she slapped her hands on her hips and glowered at her mate. "Why is everyone talking like I'm incapacitated or needing help?"

Her mate tried to hide a smile but failed miserably. "I don't know," he shrugged. "Must be a shifter thing."

Yeah, she'd show him a shifter thing or two. Luckily, her illustrated positions book was tucked safely at home. But she didn't need it anymore. She had more than enough ammo to write ten years' worth of romance—based on experience.

The End

But wait! Did you read the other books in this hot new series?
Keep reading for a preview of Caught by the Wolves and Taken by the Tiger

ABOUT THE AUTHOR

New York Times and USA Today Bestselling Author

Hi! I'm Milly Taiden. I love to write sexy stories featuring fun, sassy heroines with curves and growly alpha males with fur. My books are a great way to satisfy your craving for paranormal romance with action, humor, suspense and happily ever afters.

I live in Florida with my hubby, our son, and our fur babies: Speedy, Stormy and Teddy. I have a serious addiction to chocolate and cake.

I love to meet new readers, so come sign up for my newsletter and check out my Facebook page. We always have lots of fun stuff going on there.

SIGN UP FOR MILLY'S NEWSLETTER FOR LATEST NEWS!

http://eepurl.com/pt9q1

Find out more about Milly here:
www.millytaiden.com
milly@millytaiden.com

ALSO BY MILLY TAIDEN

Find out more about Milly Taiden here:

Email: millytaiden@gmail.com

Website: http://www.millytaiden.com

Facebook: http://www.facebook.com/millytaidenpage

Twitter: https://www.twitter.com/millytaiden

Printed in Great Britain
by Amazon

82557940R00174